**The**

"Land and S̶... or destroy each ... do it—we Sea P... Landers can't. Find them the star route. Trade them the other worlds they need, for the sea we've got to have. It's the only way, the *only* way, Johnny. Because it's not true that we're different sorts of human beings, on sea and shore. Maybe there have been sea-changes in the generations afloat—but that doesn't make them all right, and the Land all wrong. If the Land's so rotten, what was it ashore that gave birth to three thousand years of music—to three thousand years of painting, books and buildings—three thousand years of great thought and great action? I tell you they're the same, Johnny, on land and sea—the same people! Maybe with different shells of flesh and blood, but with the same human spirit in them, fighting, crying to break free!

> The star route—a pipe dream
> of peace for both Land and Sea.
> Impossible, until the strange
> contact between Johnny Joya,
> ruler of the sea, and

## THE SPACE SWIMMERS

## Also by Gordon R. Dickson:

ALIEN ART
ARCTURUS LANDING
PRO
SPACIAL DELIVERY
HOME FROM THE SHORE

*All from Ace Science Fiction*

SF

# THE SPACE
# SWIMMERS

## GORDON DICKSON

SF
ace books
**A Division of Charter Communications Inc.**
**A GROSSET & DUNLAP COMPANY**
51 Madison Avenue
New York, New York 10010

THE SPACE SWIMMERS

An ACE Book

*Cover art by: Tom Pritchett*

This Ace printing: September 1979

# THE SPACE
SWIMMERS

## GORDON DICKSON

# 1

Of the two beasts, it was the bull leopard seal
who pursued, his twelve hundred pound body
hot with rage against a barrier, a law he could not
understand. He flung himself through the gray-
green underwater of the pack ice, after the quarry
that fled before him. The leopard seal was under a
part of the ice where the taste of warning in the
water had turned him back before this. But he had
forgotten that now. The creature he followed was
neither Ross, nor crabeater, nor Weddel seal—nor
any such animal or fish he knew. It was barely
shorter than himself, furless and smooth and
gray-backed as a storm sky. —And faster than he.

It was a dolphin, a Risso's dolphin, though the
leopard seal did not know it. He only knew it did
not belong, here in his polar ocean. The only

beings his size or larger, belonging here, were the
great whales. —And the huge antarctic wolf packs
of the orcas, the killer whales, who hunted
seals—among them the leopard himself, as the
leopard seal preyed on all lesser swimmers. So it
was that the sea-leopard did not understand this
swift beast that fled so successfully from him.
—And hated it—and hunted it now to tear and kill
it.

It had been four years now since something
strange had come to live here in the white wilder-
ness of the leopard's pack ice by the Ross Shelf. It
had barred him from this, an area of his hunting
waters. Some part of his inner, living self that he
could not exactly place was angry and bruised
from the long forbidding. Killing the creature that
fled him now—here where there had been a warning to him never to hunt—would make the seal
feel better. The taste of salt blood would fill his
throat and soothe him. He would eat warm meat,
sleep on the ice in the new spring sun, and forget
strange things. Now, he chased.

The Risso's dolphin swam to escape. He was
not afraid. He knew himself to be faster than the
beast that followed. And wiser. —If it came to that
he was stronger. A twist, a dive, a sudden turn and
drive back upward at fifty miles an hour, flashing
through the water to ram his pursuer with all the
weight behind his beakless but horny nose area,
would end the chase. The blow of that beakless
front could crush and ruin the life within the
unbelievably tough, sandpaper skin of a shark.
What would it do then to the life within the little
belly fur, and warm skin, and soft fat of his fol-
lower?

Then why was it the dolphin fled? He was not sure. An instinct, a duty the leopard seal did not know, commanded him. The Risso's drove instead toward a destination earlier appointed him . . .

. . . As the year had tilted—the sixth year since the bombing of the Castle-Homes—summer had faded in the northern hemisphere and spring had grown in the south, carrying an increase of daylight. The light had strengthened, pushing back the hand of winter night which had held the antarctic pack ice off the Ross Shelf in darkness. —Under which Johnny Joya had sat for fifty-six days now, in a dim, fur-carpeted room hollowed out of a berg-chuck, mindlocked in solitary battle with the completed, self-constructed analog of a world that contained his unyielding problem— that was the world's problem as well.

It had been and was, a desperate, silent struggle, as in hand-to-hand combat, where neither fighter can gain, though every ounce of strength is poured into the fierce and straining motionlessness. So, in this struggle also, on this fifty-sixth day, Johnny was stayed, utterly still except for the faint, slow movement of his chest that showed he breathed.

His powerful swimmer's legs were clothed to the waist in the lower half of a suit of black coldwater "skins," as the undersurface garments were known among the sea-People. At his waist, almost invisible in the dimness, was a small, rectangular, flat box with a single loop of metal at each end. His body was unclothed above the waist, but in spite of the barely fifty-degree temperature of the berg-Home, his white skin showed neither gooseflesh nor bluing from the chill. It was like moonlit marble in the faint light of the short south-polar day, now filtering down through the domed ice roof overhead.

Even in dimness, his strength was apparent. His chest and arms were sculptured in power of muscle far beyond the normal even for the third generation of the sea-born. His shoulders were unusually square-boned and wide. The deltoid muscles humped out toward the clavicles; and the heavy pectoral muscles, relaxed, creased downward over the lower rib cage. The belly area was one concave wall of muscle.

The heavy forearms and long-fingered, square-palmed hands lay relaxed on the black-clad knees. The face was tilted toward the dark brown-gray of the Weddel seal fur under the black-clothed feet. The level brows were dark, below the dark brown of the hair and above the straight nose, straight mouth, and square chin. Under those brows, the blue eyes in this moment were darkened by the intense concentration of the mind behind them; like lamps dimmed by the drain of the power that fed them, to serve some heavy need elsewhere. They did not move.

Behind the eyes, the mind was elsewhere. In the analog—a place, but not here. Six years had passed since the bombing of the Castle-Homes that had been the undersurface cities of the sea-People; and in one of which his wife had died.— Five years since he had brought his then five year old son to this berg-Home. Nine days more than four years since he had begun translating his problem into terms of the massive, mental counterpart of the force-filled universe, with which he now wrestled. Fifty-six days since the analog had been completed.

And for fifty-six days now it had resisted him, refusing to give up any translated image of the world outside the berg-Home that would contain a relevancy to his problem. For fifty-six days he had been blocked, at a standstill; like a man trying to walk ahead through a stone wall against which he already stands spread-eagled.

But the thought of relaxing the effort of his search, even on this fifty-sixth day, never occurred to him. He was the instinctive leader of the sea-born third-generation. Therefore, his leading should have led them only to better things.

It had not. Six years ago, his leadership had brought about only the bombing of the Castle-Homes and the outlawry of the People—so that anyone of the Land who cared to might now hunt them down in the seas, like animals, for sport.

Therefore, in his leading there had been an error. That error remained. —But alone with his son, apart, isolated in the pack ice, he still remained instinctive leader of his People. That could not be changed—therefore the error must be found and corrected.

So the determination to find it was not a matter subject to internal debate. Nor was it even something peculiar to the sea-born. Even with land-birth, Johnny might have possessed it. —But the idea of seeking it by means of the immense mental construction that was the analog of all operative forces on sea and shore, this four-dimensional darkness filled with forces through which his mind moved in search of an answer, that was an

idea possible only to a mature individual possess-
ing all the peculiar instincts and perceptions of
the third-generation sea-born humans.

Also, only with the talents of the third generation, could Johnny, now that the analog was constructed, view what was to be seen in it—the mul-
tiplicity of literal mind's eye images of events
now happening beyond the berg-Home walls, on
land and in the sea.

It was not with a clairvoyance that he saw these,
nor with any extrasensory perception, in the ordinary sense. For he did not see in order to know.
Rather he knew, in his third-generation calculations from the forces in the analog, what must be
at any point in contemporaneous time and space.
And therefore saw for efficiency's sake.

But, for all his ability to visualize from the
analog, the overwhelming number of images possible to him baffled his search. There was a human
limit—even to one of the third generation—of the
number of images he could examine at one time
for a relevancy to the error he sought.

There were too many to view at once, even
within that sub-class of available images that related to him personally.

Like the life-and-death pursuit at this moment
taking place beneath the polar ice, not two sea
miles from where he sat.

—Yet, this particular image was relevant.


. . . . The Risso's dolphin fled. The sea leopard
followed close. Hunted and hunter, they flew as if
in an underwater ballet along the vast white face
of a submerged, vertical wall of ice. It was the side
of a berg-chunk, the edge of a great piece of pan

ice, and it stretched along beneath the open water for over a hundred yards before its smooth face was broken by the entrance to an underwater bay.

The dolphin swung into this bay. It was too large beyond the entrance for its walls to be seen, and in it, enclosed by the ice, the light was dimmer. The seal, following close, entered also. —And checked.

The quarry at last had turned to face him. But it was not alone any longer. Beside it now was a strange, black, upright, four-limbed figure. A round, transparent something glittered like ice on the front of its head. There were wide black fin-shapes at the end of its lower limbs and something long and separate was held in the ends of its upper limbs. It faced the leopard seal. And, at the same time, below them all in the depths of the ice bay, the seal sensed, rather than saw, the great, dark-backed, rising shape of a thirty-five foot male killer whale.

"Leave here, Leopard!"

—The boyish human voice was distorted, coming from the dark, membrane-covered opening at the base of the glittering roundness. But this made no difference, for the words had no meaning for the seal. Only the message of command in the young voice, clear-pitched and calm, came plain to the beast through the most primitive fibers of his being. His mouth and lungs were closed against the water pressure, but his soul snarled defiance.

"No," answered the voice, thin-sounding in the heavy medium of the water where sound waves had three times the speed they achieved in the air-filled throat and glinting mask. "This is my sea, here! Leopards and wild killers stay clear!"

The seal hung balanced in the water. Rage, and the mortal threats of the voice and the killer whale, teetered against each other in his inflamed and furious soul.

"You've tasted the warnings in these waters!" came the voice through the dim water. "Turn around, Leopard—and go."

The seal remembered the opening in the ice at his back. He saw the killer whale now, drifting upward. He saw the dolphin poised, and the black creature that was a ten year old boy in a skin-tight, coldwater suit and waterlung. —And the fuse of his frustration and fury burnt short and blew all reason from his mind.

His doglike muzzle wrinkled in berserk rage. But even before it wrinkled, before the nerve and muscle reflex was accomplished that drove him with all the strength of his wide hind flippers at the black figure of his enemy, even as he died, a little light winked in the end of the thing his enemy held—and that was all he saw. The light expanded suddenly into a brilliance that lit all the inside of his head; and the golden flame of his anger burst like a flaring meteor into darkness, as the powerful blow of the sonic rifle struck into his brain along the lance of light from the rifle's sighting mechanism, exploding the gray cells in his skull and ending the beating of his heart.

Tomi Joya moved aside in the water as the eleven-foot leopard-spotted shape slid past him, turning a little on its side, aimlessly slowing as the mass of the water stopped it.

"No, Conquistador!" said the boy, as the killer whale rose like a dark-backed storm cloud through the water, trailing the several reins from the straps he wore—like a harness around his great body in front of the tall, black dorsal fin that rose like a triangular sail from his mid-back. "I want his pelt. Then you can have him. Come here."

The killer drifted close.

"He was brave, Conquistador," said Tomi, as he reached out to secure the drifting body with one of the reins, tight to the killer's harness. "But he got too far in before we stopped him. No leopards are to come here. No leopards and no wild killers! You hear me, Conquistador? —Baldur?"

His voice beat upward on the last words to a note of command, the maturity of which rang strangely at odds with the youthfulness of the voice itself. Killer whale and dolphin drifted away from him on either side, without visible swimming motions.

"No . . ." said Tomi, contritely. He caught one of the reins of the killer and reached out his hand through the water to the dolphin. Both beasts returned to him until his hands touched their smooth sides. "I know . . . I know the wild killers never come now, and the leopards only when they get wild mad like this one. But my dad still gets to thinking when he swims around, and forgets his rifle, sometimes. It's for him. You know . . . You know . . ." He stroked the two cetaceans soothingly. I have to keep them all happy and in balance, he thought—and his hands paused. *Balance*—it was a new thought . . .

His voice became brisk once more.

"Home now!" he said. "Home, Conquistador. Baldur!"

The boxcar length of the killer whale turned and left the ice bay, towing the dead leopard seal and Tomi. The dolphin followed. They went out and up to the surface of an opening in the ice pack, breathed through the blowholes in the top of their cetacean heads—and so continued, diving and breathing, by the undulating three-dimensional pathways of their kind to a large, free-floating small berg two sea miles off.

Here they dove under the berg until they came to the mouth of a dark tunnel leading directly upward and too small for the killer to enter. Untying the dead seal, Tomi and the dolphin pushed it into the tunnel opening and rose upward toward dim light above. Forty feet up, they emerged with it into a weirdly blue-lit chamber hollowed out of the berg itself. Their heads broke through the surface of the water. They had come up to sea level within the ice. Tomi clambered out of the water onto the surrounding ice floor of the chamber. Reaching down, he took hold of the fur and loose skin at the neck of the dead seal.

It was a casual, automatic, everyday action, of the sort taken for granted by the boy himself and the dolphin—even by the killer whale outside the berg-chunk, and the man silent in his thoughts—had they too been watching. But in it was implicit all that difference in Tomi that separated him from every other human being in the world—even the other scattered, hunted children of his own sea-born fourth generation.

And it contained the clue to that error which his father sought, as well as the potential means of its correction.

# 2

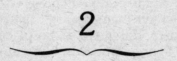

Tomi's hands gripped hard on the loose and furry skin at the dead seal's neck.

"Push, Baldur!" he said to the protruding head of the dolphin. His voice echoed strangely through the diaphragm of his mask here in the dim, air-filled chamber. Baldur dipped his head below the surface, put his hard muzzle against the seal's body and drove it upward, while the boy hauled. The body slid out on the ice and lay there.

Even allowing for the nearly frictionless slope of the ice at the pool's edge and the thrust of the big dolphin, pulling over half a ton of dead animal weight from the water was an incredible feat of strength for a ten-year-old boy—even one already as tall and well-muscled as most men. But Tomi Joya did it without thought, as a boy his age might

heave a large sack of groceries through a doorway,
ashore.

He stood up now, wearing the water-lung mask
and black coldwater skins that covered him completely. At his waist was a duplicate of the rectangular box with the two end loops that his father
was wearing—the generator of that magnetic
pressure-envelope that in the water enclosed him
like a second suit, deflecting at right angles to its
immaterial surface any uniform pressure brought
against it. Even the pressure of the ocean's
greatest five and six mile depths. With this, and
the mask which manufactured oxygen for him
from the surrounding water, no place in the sea
was barred to him—and this, like many things, he
took for granted.

He was not aware that he was in any way unusual. He took for granted also all the messages
brought him by the stirring waters. —As he took
for granted the fact that Conquistador and Baldur
both understood and obeyed him; and that even
the wild killer whales, that could have swallowed
him at a gulp, listened when he spoke to them and
steered clear of his waters. His authority over the
wild orcs was not in the fact that he could have
shot and killed any one of them before the first
twitch of mighty flukes drove them at him. The
untamed killers cruised around him in the open
water like thirty-foot wolves as he spoke, and
together in their packs they were physically his
superior. Also, they were those from whom everything in the sea fled, and they were not used to
fear. Yet, there was something about him that
daunted them. The boy was not afraid of them, he

spoke to and understood them, and he ordered them as a ruler orders his servants. Somewhere from all these things along his deep, strange, and different channel of communication with them came a half-hidden, incomprehensible knowledge that awed them, like a superstition.

"This is my sea, here," he told them. "You will stay clear." And they agreed that it was his sea, not theirs, and went. They were more intelligent than the leopard seals and their awe was greater. Once told, they kept their distance.

Now, the seal body lay draining salt water from its coarse fur down the sloped ice back into the pool. Tomi pushed back the transparent circle of his waterlung mask and breathed deep.

He was now filling his lungs with the air of the berg-Home. He could hear the faint beating of the roomlung that replenished that air with oxygen extracted from the water of the pool, as his waterlung extracted it when he swam outside. The thermonuclear fusion unit that powered the room lung was a large model of the tiny one in his waterlung. Both were devices developed by the sea-People and these, too, Tomi also took for granted along with the heat, light, and all other services of the berg-Home powered by the unit.

But he was not concerned with such things, any more than he was concerned with the awe of the wild killers. What concerned him instead was the mystery and wonder of his father's silent mental struggle here in the berg-Home during the last few years. In the clear understanding of his own instincts and awarenesses, Tomi had come from the little area and small battles of the waters outside to a vast place where titanic, if unreal, forces moved, here in this small, dim, ice-enclosed room. He looked about it now.

The lights were off. Around Tomi there was only the gloomily faint, blue illumination of sunlight, filtered through the thick ice over the berg-Home. Now that his eyes were adjusting, Tomi made out the different colors of the furs of Ross and Weddel seal covering the floor area, the dome-shaped ice walls and room, and the wide-shouldered, motionless shape of his father, seated on the fur-covered ten-foot length of the underwater sea-sled.

Tomi had already reached out to switch on the light control box that would flood the interior of the berg-Home with sun like illumination. But now his hand checked. His father, he saw, was utterly motionless; and from the library unit's black box at the man's feet, Tomi made out the sounding of a thin wisp of melody. It was the Moho Symphony, written by Johnny's first cousin, Patrick Joya—now self-exiled from the outlawed sea-People and a renegade ashore.

Tomi's hand dropped. He took three steps across the floor to stand beside the sled, looking down from the side at the still, strong-boned face of his father. Now, the boy saw how under the thick, dark brows the blue eyes in this moment were darkened by their intense concentration— and the exciting thought of all things, all creatures, all movements being held somehow in *balance* returned with sudden, beckoning, compelling force to Tomi's mind.

Tomi breathed noiselessly and carefully, watching and feeling.

The invisible, impalpable tension about his father, as of some great endeavor, was stronger this time than the boy had ever felt it before. Now it seemed, to Tomi's sensitive fourth-generation perceptions, to be even closer than ever to a break-point, to some final moment of decision that would echo out from this berg-Home when it came, over all the world, across all the universe.

The thought about *balance* moved in Tomi.

Silently, with the skill of long practice, and the idea of balance thrilling inside him, the boy sank cross-legged to the furs on the ice floor, still watching his father. Smoothly and quietly, he laid his forearms on the thighs of his crossed legs as his father's forearms lay on the black-clad, adult legs. Tomi leaned forward slightly from the waist. His shoulders slumped, his head bowed in imitation of the man. So perfect was the mimicry that to the gaze of the watching dolphin, superstitious like his killer whale cousins, an eerie sort of magic seemed to flow from the larger human figure to the smaller, remolding the latter.

Before Baldur's eyes, the face of the young boy slowly changed, in a way that was different from any way the dolphin had ever seen it change before.

As Baldur watched, Tomi's features seemed to draw in on themselves. They leaned and harshened, with a maturity too old for them. The boy's eyes focused on the dark fur pelt beyond the pillars of his knees, until he saw only the darkness of the fur and the darkness seemed to flow up to take possession of his thoughts. Now, in darkness, he began to move mentally into the unreal place that occupied his father.

It was not Tomi's first visit to this place, nor had he found his way to it by the route of his father. Nor by telepathy, nor any means any other living human might have taken. Only and uniquely, by his own strange individual ability to communicate and by an imitation of Johnny so primitive and deep that it went clear back to the protozoan consciousness. By this path, long since, Tomi had come to the area of his father's silent struggle and though he had never let the man know it for fear of being forbidden, he had joined Johnny in his search.

Now, however, as he sank further this time into the force-laden darkness, Tomi felt a new urge thrilling inside him. It was the recent idea of *balance* . . . but of something greater than ordinary balance. He felt it now; not driving him, as in the past, down into the analog; but upward and outward from it, into a vaster region.

For the first time he noticed that many of the forces that applied within the area of the analog, passed up and beyond it—outward into immensity, where other, greater forces also struck and joined and moved. Eagerly, he followed outward, also, leaving the analog area behind; and slowly, then quickly, it seemed to him that the general darkness was beginning to lighten.

But it was not a lightening like that from sunlight, but like that of some different illumination. He came out of the darkness into it at last; into a strange, vast, *balanced* place where glowing golden lines like girders seemed to stretch away into unguessable distances, like parts of some immense, inconceivable construction.

—And huge, living, singing shapes flashed

along the girders at a speed too great for him to follow.

Forgetful, now, even of his father's problem, fascinated, Tomi's own perception flashed off along the girders in pursuit of the singing shapes. —But without success. Like an ant, lost among the metal bones of some mighty building, in pursuit of butterflies, he scurried this way and that, further and further, until all thought of return was lost to him in the heat of the chase.

Watching, worried, fearful, in the ice pool of the berg-Home, the dolphin Baldur saw the light in the boy's eyes dwindle toward extinction. Fear surged up in Baldur. He lifted his head from the pool and cried out—the long, weeping whistle, falling in tone at the end, that is the distress cry of the dolphin people.

The boy never stirred to the sound of it.

But Johnny stirred. Baldur was sea-friend to the father as Conquistador the killer whale was sea-friend to the son—and the bonds of sea-friendship went deep. Even in the depths of his own concentration, Johnny heard the call for help and came slowly back to the berg-Home.

He raised his head, looked around—and saw Tomi, still as a statue of black ice.

Johnny froze, immobile himself as the berg-Home walls around him. Suddenly and with shock he understood what his son was doing— and what the boy must have done on many similar occasions before this. Alarmed, Johnny stretched out his hand instinctively to wake the boy with a touch on one dark-clothed young shoulder—

—And all search ended.

For, in the fractional second of touching, something like a spark jumped between their two egos—a double-working of that quality of communication that Tomi so unselfconsciously but uniquely, possessed.

In that moment, contact was made from both sides.

Suddenly Johnny, with his son, was out beyond the analog, in the vaster place of golden girders. And at once the understanding he had been seeking leaped upon him; he saw his error. Finally, it came, in the recognition of something the boy could not have recognized. —The identity of the singing shapes Tomi was pursuing without success. They were those whom Johnny himself had pursued, once in a spaceship, together with other sea-born Cadets of the Space Academy of the Land.

Pursued—and killed, under the brutal misdirected research methods of the Academy in its search for the secret of faster-than-light travel which the shapes possessed. For these were the great Space Swimmers—space-born, void-dwelling creatures of living gas within living magnetic fields to whom the Landers had given the old horror name of "Space Bats." A name which like their research methods had betrayed their lack of perceptive understanding of the creatures as the sea-born instinctively understood them.

That betrayal had also betrayed their lack of understanding of the sea-born themselves. To Johnny, even then leader of his generation and his People, had come the sudden perceptive understanding that the sea-and land-born must separate—or clash. And so he had led the sea-born Cadets back to the oceans.

But the Land, not understanding, had demanded their return, for the Landers did not have the sea-born sensitivities for spatial research planned for the Swimmers by the Land. When Johnny had refused, the Leaders ashore had bombed the Castle-Homes, and made a law that the sea-People were now outside the law, to be hunted like animals in the sea by any one who cared to do so. And all that had led to this . . .

But now Johnny saw the great Swimmers of Space again, through his son's perceptions. And understanding showed him clearly now where he had gone wrong six years ago.

His error had lain hidden then, fifty-six days within a very human spot of blindness in Johnny himself. As any parent might, he had forgotten all this time to notice the days and years of his son's growing. Now, suddenly, he stood face to face with the abilities of the fourth-generation sea-born, not as possibilities in a four year old child, but as actualities living in the ten year old body under his hand.

And at once the error was plain and obvious. It had been the fourth, not the third generation, who would have been equipped to win out the inevitable clash with the Land. Johnny, by bringing the Cadets home, and then refusing to return, had brought about the conflict between sea and shore one generation too soon.

. . . By doing so—now, with the analog corrected, the answer stood stark before his mind's eye—he had set off a slide toward Armageddon between land and sea. He had lit four separate fuses of action six years past, any one of which could light the final explosion within six months from now—before the year tilted from antarctic spring back to antarctic fall again.

Two fuses burned ashore, proclaimed the analog. One, in the depths of the sea. And one—in sea on shore.

And the only way Johnny could hope to prevent the explosion now, was to beat all four fuses to their end—to win the test of sea against land before its time—within the next six months.

But only an adult of Tomi's fourth generation—read the analog—could hope to win; and Tomi, oldest of his generation, was still ten years from his maturity.

There was no hope then . . . Yes, there was one. Johnny's face grew still in thought.

He could gamble; there was still time for that. It was one thing to extrapolate the present. No one could extrapolate the future with its infinite possibilities springing from each action. Yet, odds could be calculated. Like a navigator starting out to circumnavigate a globe, one could calculate from point to point across the chartless sea of possibilities.

He could attempt to combine his own third-generation maturity with the still half-hidden talents of the fourth, in Tomi—and together they could gain control of events on sea and shore.

It was only a chance—but there was no other. And, even from the first, he must begin to sacrifice much of what he had gained. It was only his position outside the events duplicated in the analog that had allowed him to read it like this in clear images. Now, he must step back into that stream of action from which he had stood aside; and once within its current, he would be unable to view it dispassionately and accurately as he had from outside.

For the last time, then . . . Johnny closed his eyes and reached into the analog for that image most useful to his first step down into the wild current of events.

—Sharp as vision could make it, an image formed. It was a clear sight of the tall, lean figure of his cousin, Patrick Joya, now six years self-exiled ashore; and once, after Johnny's now dead wife and Tomi, the closest of all the sea-People to Johnny.

Pat was descending from an air-shuttle bus at a coastal terminal. His thin face bore deeper lines than had marked it six years ago and his eyes were darkened and weary. But their pupils were pale and steady with purpose. They looked, unseeing, in Johnny's direction; and, as Johnny watched, he saw Pat striding toward him . . . .

# 3

In that moment of Johnny's perception—eight thousand miles away—Patrick Joya, ashore, stepped from the air-shuttle onto the balcony level of the main Terminal Building at Savannah Stand, Georgia. Towering with his sea-born height and lean body a full head above the tallest of the other shuttle passengers, he stood still for a second, letting them move away from around him. He glanced skyward through the invisible weather shield of the roofless Terminal. So far, he thought, nothing. And no one who knew him had encountered him.

An hour since, at Entertainment Estates North on Lake of the Woods, Pat had felt the first sharpness of Canadian winter in the air. He had heard the wild, gray Canada geese calling, flying to the south; and the music that was always in him had answered back to them with the single, low, clear note of an oboe. He had seen the sugar maples burning red and yellow among the dark green of spruce and pine, above the black water of the lake. He had felt the year turn, advancing beneath him—and all the great, single unity of race and purpose that had guided all the music he had ever written, and had driven him to turn even against his own sea-born People, came back upon him.

It had sent him in the past even against the decision of Johnny, whom all of the third generation of the sea followed with an instinct as pure as that which had led the geese then flying in formation behind their leader. But he did not doubt his belief, even now after six years of self-exile ashore. For at any moment such as then, when he had cared to stop and listen, he could feel in himself the beating of the heart of the world through time and space—that told him he was right. He had been right. He was still right. And he must continue on his chosen lonely path.

Now, however, here, two thousand miles south and east and one hour later, by sighing vacuum subway express under the carpet of homes that hid the surface of the continent's southern part too thickly for roads to exist, the dark and lowering skies over the warm and sticky air of the southern shore showed that—even here, though differently—the summer was ending. And the hour of decision, he thought, approaching.

Turning his head slowly about as he stood, he scanned the sagging, gray, cloud-belly of those skies. From sea-horizon to the sharp-edged, modern buildings of Savannah Complex, inland, he saw nothing. Nothing but the byzantine-cross shapes, like crossed dumbbells, of a few ducted-fan charter flyers leaving or returning to their ranks, down on the ramp overhanging the sea-waves at the foot of the Terminal Building.

He glanced at the watch on his wrist. He had twelve minutes to kill. To get down to the main floor, cross it, enter the flyers' ranks and walk to the end of them, would take no more than five. He strode forward around an angled section of wall that hid him from the shuttle landing area and the people coming in from the subway terminal at Savannah Complex. Before him was only the bal-cony railing. He leaned on the top rail and looked down at the butterfly crowd swarming the main floor, forty feet below. None of the thousands of people he saw there were wasting a glance on the heavy skies above. Even here, in transit and sup-posedly at leisure, they were wrapped up and concentrated in their continual one-upmanship struggle for social superiority and prestige, ironi-cally named The Game. The Game—to which even an individual's work was secondary, nowa-days, ashore.

They milled about the aisles between the roof-less seating areas, bars, shops, and restaurants in the gaudy extravagances of their clothing. Their artificial perfumes struggled with the perfumes of the roses, the early tulips, and late-blooming as-ters all in flower simultaneously about them. They passed beneath the trimmed orange trees that were shaking down their blossoms to mingle with the white petals snowed from the apple trees along the aisles. Their perfumes, the smells of the flowers around them, mingled with the feverish heat of their bodies and rose to the balcony to stun the nose of Pat. The oddly sharp, deep lines prematurely graven in his still face grew deeper, and his mouth went thin and straight, with disgust.

The sharp-toned, competitive, clashing of their voices in the echoing Terminal was thrown back, repeated, and blended at last into a soughing like the sound of the sea. The tympanous discordance of it faded in Pat's mind into the hush and mutter of the waves; and, as memory came back riding the remembered sound, his eyes shadowed, the thinness went from his lips. And once more he felt the life of the world beating whole and strong within him.

"—Hello, Pat," said a familiar, soft, but oddly ringing voice of a man behind him. "Watching the players in The Game of Life, are you?"

Pat turned, smoothly. His sea-born nerves were too healthy to betray him with a nervous start. Just inside the screening wall stood Barth Stuve— Stu-*vay*, the name was pronounced—President, or "baron" in popular slang, of the Construction Group. A short, slim, but strangely arresting figure in one of his ridiculously wide-shouldered fur jackets sporting the yellow plumb bob emblem that was the trademark of his Group. He smiled a little ironic smile, at Pat.

Pat nodded back—unsmiling and looking steadily at him. Even after these six, long, unbroken years on shore it was hard for him to believe a single man like this could represent the pinnacle of success to the two hundred million stockholder-employees, wearing the plumb bob Mark, who were in any way concerned with construction in the world. —And that this single small but brilliant individual could be one of only ten such Group leaders, who made up the Council that in fact ruled the three billion people of the land. In the thick jacket of sable fur with the air-conditioning collar required to make it comfortable in this summer temperature, that made Pat's summer slacks and shirt normal wear, Stuve looked top-heavy and unnatural as the plumb bob of his jacket Mark. There was a rumor that he wore such jackets to hide some deformity—that in fact he was a hunchback.

Pat found it hard to believe. A man like Stuve would be more likely to show such a disability openly, turning it into a Mark of his own, a badge of difference. No, if there was anything crooked about Barth Stuve, Baron of Construction, it was more likely to be in his mind than in his body. A great player of The Game according to reputation—was Stuve.

"You don't like that name for the people down there?" went on the smaller man now. He continued to smile at Pat. Under a high forehead his dark eyes were so deeply set that the skin seemed shadowed to blackness beneath them. Below that blackness his face was fine-boned, straight-nosed and -mouthed, firm-chinned—almost handsome.

"Neither the name nor The Game," said Pat.

"But you're a composer, a maker, that's why," said Stuve, softly. "You're not involved. Anyway, when I saw you here, I thought I'd find you looking up, not down. Looking for a Space Bat."

"Space Bat?" For a moment Pat did not understand. Then he remembered the old Lander horror-name for the Space Swimmers.

"Hadn't you heard? One was seen over Berlin

Complex, forty or fifty minutes ago—followed by public panic and forecasts of judgment day. That makes a dozen seen in the last month, and there's talk passing around that the Bats are getting ready for revenge on us; for all of them you sea-People in the Space Academy killed, studying them, at Academy orders, of course—six to ten years ago." The dark eyes studied Pat, alertly. "You don't know anything about it?"

"No," said Pat.

"And it doesn't interest you—any more than The Game does. That it?" Stuve laughed lightly. His voice was baritone, but as soft as velvet. "Anyway, it wasn't Space Bats or The Game I stepped over to speak to you about when I saw you here. I thought I'd pass you the word—you're free of surveillance, at last."

"Am I?" Pat gazed down at him. "Thanks."

"Don't thank me. Kai Ebberly proposed it— though I suppose your own Baroness, Mila Jhan, put him up to it. She probably thought it better not to propose it herself—since you're in her Entertainment Group."

"She didn't say anything to me about doing it," said Pat.

"Maybe—she wanted to surprise you." Stuve smiled again. This time there was something a little lewd about that smile. Pat ignored it.

"Who disagreed?" he asked.

"With Ebberly proposing?" Stuve laughed again—out loud, if softly. "He's King of the Castle, Pat. You don't object to propositions from the Transportation Baron, Pat. His Group's half again as big as mine, remember—and mine's the next biggest."

"But you say he did what Mila asked?" Pat gazed intently at Stuve.

"Oh—" said Stuve, waving a long-fingered, supple hand, "he'd have his reasons, or he wouldn't do it. Maybe he still hopes to get your sea-People to give him Cadets again; now that the land Cadets are so useless they've shut the Academy down. Maybe he still aims to get the Space Swimmers' secret of a faster-than-light drive and explore the stars. Who knows? —Who knows?" Stuve's eyes darkened and became almost invisible in their deep sockets. "He's not out of The Game, just because he's top man in the world."

"Maybe you're wrong," said Pat, grimly. "Maybe he's too big for it."

Stuve shook his head.

"No," said Stuve, "there's more to The Game, and what it takes, than you realize—than anyone realizes. Never mind— You're out of it, Pat." He smiled suddenly, almost impishly. "Or are you—? Well, we won't worry about it. How about coming along with me and the crew I've got waiting downstairs there?" He gestured behind him. "We're going to Australia. Melbourne—for the races."

"Thanks," said Pat. "I've got an appointment."

"Yes . . . well," Stuve started to turn away. "As I say, that's your trouble, you creative people. You work too much. Well, there'll be another—" he broke off, idly, and swung back to face Pat. "I don't suppose you've any idea . . ." he hesitated, "any idea if your cousin's alive or dead, these days?"

"Cousin?"

"Johnny Joya. The one who led the Cadets back to the sea and started the sea-revolt."

"I haven't been in the sea for six years," said Pat, flatly. "You know that."

"No . . . I suppose not," said Stuve, slowly. "It's too bad. I always thought your cousin would have been one man worth talking to. He always sounded interesting to me."

He broke off.

"Well," he said. "You've got your appointment, and I've got Melbourne race track waiting. Come see me when you've got time."

"When I've got time," said Pat. He saw the top-heavy figure vanish around the wall's edge and looked at his watch. He had used eight of his twelve minutes. Far from being long on time, now he was short of it.

He quitted the balcony, took the escalator ramp toward the main level below and pushed through the crowd toward the doorway at the sea-end of the building that was his destination. The aisles were crowded everywhere, except around a small glassed-in display stand he passed. On the stand, ignored by all the raucous crowds, was a gold-plated device looking like a piece of abstract sculpture put together out of a plumber's box of odds and ends. It was the life-size model of the automatic interstellar probe started across the four light-years of space to Alpha Centauri, nearest planet-like star to Earth, in a burst of enthusiasm that had been world-wide, once, only a dozen years before.

The sight of it stirred him once more with a memory of the sea so poignant it was like a sharp, physical pain in his chest. He shook the emotion

from him, went on stepping out through a doorway into a warm, damp day with a little wind
blowing and the clouds overhead flowing swiftly
inland from the sea.

Fifteen feet outside the doorway was a tall wire
fence pierced by a gate at which stood a guard
who was outsize for the land-born. He was as tall
as Pat and outweighed Pat by a good fifty pounds.
He was a big young man with an open face under
untidy black hair. But the easy grin on his lips did
not reach up to his eyes. His eyes were squinted,
and shadowed underneath as if from lack of sleep.

He wore the blue interlocked wheels of the
Transportation Mark on his shirt, and he glanced
at the twin masks of the Entertainment Group,
laughing and crying on the pocket of Pat's shirt, as
Pat came up.

He moved to block the doorway in the fence, but
stood aside again as Pat handed him several of the
little, extra-legal wafers of gold stamped with the
mark of one or another of the Groups, and known
as "chips." These were the only thing approaching untraceable money on the computer-run land,
where getting and spending alike were matters of
credit cards and recorded, automatic bookkeep-
ing. He tucked the chips Pat gave him into a pocket of his slacks, but as Pat stepped by, he reached
out and caught Pat's arm.

"Wait a minute," he said. "Don't I know you?
You're Joya, the renegade composer from the sea.
It ought to be worth more to you than four chips to
get down next to the ocean without anyone knowing you're there."

Pat looked at him. The big young man smiled,

showing white, regular teeth and held tight to
Pat's left arm.

Pat reached across with his right hand and took
hold of the forearm just above the hand that held
him. Pat's long, spatulate fingers, powered with
the innately greater strength of those born and
raised in the sea—and developed beyond even
that strength by twenty years of daily exercise on
piano and stringed instruments—sank in between
the bones of the ulna and radius.

The guard grunted and dropped to his knees,
his face going white. His helpless, grasping hand
fluttered from its hold on Pat's arm.

"If you knew that much about me," said Pat
softly, "you'd know I wouldn't be here in broad
daylight bribing you with chips if it weren't simply easier than getting a pass to go through this
gate. Why try such a thing?"

"Just playing The Game—" gasped the guard,
"for God's sake—my arm—. "

"Some people aren't in your Game," said Pat.
With a sudden jerk of his wrist he threw the guard
sprawling on the clean-swept, gray concrete of
the pavement. "Next time," he said, "remember
that."

He left the man huddled on the pavement, nurs-
ing his arm, and walked through the gate, down
between the first and second ranks of the ducted-
fan flyers. The dark-jacketed pilots, standing
around or fiddling with their flyers, waiting to be
called up to the taxi entrance around the front of
the Terminal, glanced idly at him passing by, but
looked away immediately again.

It was not unusual to see strangers slipping

through the gate, so that when they chartered one of the flyers payment could be made in chips instead of in a traceable assignment of credit. Looking between the flyers of the first rank, Pat could see the gray, choppy surface of the sea, lapping at the concrete pier on which the flyers were ranked. The tide was in and the water came within three feet of the wheels of the front rank flyers.

Pat looked ahead to the end of the ranks. The ranks stretched long and there was another hundred yards to walk. He glanced at his watch and walked a little faster. Without warning, he passed a gap between two flyers in the front rank and saw a craft there that was not in the usual shape of a flyer—the dumbbell-shaped hull matched by the bulge of a ducted fan inside its circular housing on each side of the middle body. This other craft was dart-shaped, with small, back-raked wings and heavy jet tubes in the rear. It was a dull red in color, with not the interlocked wheels of the Transportation Group but the plumb bob of Stuve's Construction Group, yellow on its side.

Pat turned his head away quickly. A short round-faced man with a heavy brown mustache was talking to a man who was obviously a professional Hunter. The ship was a Hunter ship, of the kind used by those who made a sport of chasing and capturing or killing the now outlawed sea-People. But it was not this that made Pat hurry by. It was the fact that he recognized the short brown-mustached man as a distant relative of Stuve's. Pat had seen him at a party given at Construction Estates South in Brazil, less than a month before. He had remembered the man because of the deformed upper lip that the thick mustache did an unsuccessful job of hiding.

The brown mustache turned toward him now as the man glanced idly in Pat's direction. For a moment Pat thought he had been recognized in turn, but the other's gaze moved on to look back up toward the Terminal Building. Putting his head down, Pat went on swiftly. He was almost to the end of the ranked flyers, where the pier on which they stood butted a concrete angle into the choppy, warm, gray waters.

He glanced at his watch again. It was full on fifteen minutes past fifteen hundred hours. He looked ahead, into the sullen horizon where the lead-colored sea met the heavy sky. But there was no shape outlined against it, no touch of color that might grow to the shape of a Space Swimmer.

The last of the flyers and the end of the pier were only a few yards away. Unnecessarily, to Pat's mind came suddenly the timetable of all the appearances of Space Swimmer shapes over the crowded land in the last six months. He smiled a little, tightly. Before that they had been seen by no one except the Space Academy personnel and Cadets, who had hunted them beyond the sun orbit of Earth. And that seeing had ceased when the sea-Cadets, revolting against such hunting that always ended in the suicide of the Swimmers, had ended the research by leaving the Academy behind Johnny Joya. No wonder the sudden sight of the Swimmers over the cities of Earth this last year had disturbed and frightened even this modern generation of the land. —Though there was no sensible basis for fear. For all their vast shapes—

like waving gossamer curtains half a mile wide—
the weight of the living Swimmers could be calculated in ounces, in Earth's gravitational field.

But it had never been thought that the space-
born creatures could come into the Earth's atmosphere. Nor could they. Pat's smile at this thought
grew thin and bitter. But the great flying shapes
had been seen and the old, emotional horror-
name of Space Bat revived.

But here he was at the end of the pier, and there
was nothing to be seen in the sky but a few of the
ducted-fan flyers. He could not stand here long
without one of the pilots around the ranks asking
him what he wanted. Tautly, Pat lifted his head to
scan the southern sky again and this time he saw
it.

A darkly bluish shape, seeming to flicker
against the gray clouds. Perhaps ten miles off, but
coming at several times the speed of sound.

Pat glanced around him. No one on the pier had
seen it yet. He looked back up into the sky. It was
swelling rapidly. Now he could see it undulating
like a wide piece of cloth carried along on a moving current of water. —Voices began suddenly to
rise behind him. The babble swelled to a mounting groan of panic, a moan that went racing like a
cresting wave back toward the Terminal where
the thousands there would be lifting their gaze
skyward now.

The Swimmer came on, dipped low and
seemed to fill most of the blue sky with its massive
half-mile spread of dark, rippling surface. It
seemed to be swooping on the Terminal, as if to
swallow it up.

The sky darkened further. Pat glanced around.

No one was looking his way now. Pilots were running up the pier, away from the falling dark blue shadow. He went swiftly around to the far side of the last flyer in the front rank and found himself alone with the corner of concrete, the sky, and the sea. He reached into his pocket and took out a thick, black collar with a small box attached to its front and above this a transparent face mask. It was the waterlung that, together with a message from the sea, had been delivered to him four days before.

He clipped the collar around his throat and pressed the mask over his face, where it clung as if glued. With a final glance around to make sure he was still unobserved, he turned and went quietly over the edge of the concrete into the chopping waves two feet below.

He slipped under the gray, shadow-darkened surface of the water and a little line of bubbles from the collar of the device marked his going. He did not surface again; and soon the bubbles he left behind burst, and were lost among the tossing small peaks of the waves, headed out to sea.

# 4

Half a mile offshore, and twelve feet—two fathoms—below the surface of the sea, a quicksilver dolphin-shape some eighteen feet in length and looking like a canoe with a transparent hood running from stem to stern, appeared suddenly out of the green dimness of the water and slid to a stop beside Pat.

The heat of its steam jets created a momentary warmth in the water around him, and a section of the transparent hood slid back, leaving only the iridescent film of a magnetic pressure envelope holding back the sea. Pat pushed through it into the air-filled cockpit and sat down in the open rear seat of the two-man smallboat, just ahead of the small steam chamber and the deuterium fusion unit that powered it, changing scooped-up sea-water to superheated steam that jetted the flimsy craft through the underseas at speeds approaching two hundred knots. The long-jawed man in the front cockpit, Pat saw, was Martin Connor—an ex-Cadet of the third generation, and an old friend of Johnny and Pat as well.

"Followed?" asked Martin now, looking back over his shoulder. Pat was jarred to see the lines in Martin's face that had not been there six years before.

"I don't think so," said Pat. "But I can't be sure."

"We'll go deep." Martin touched the control board before him. The transparent section above Pat slid back into place, the smallboat tilted and plunged down through the water like an aircraft in a power dive. The light faded abruptly about them . . . and then seemed to return slowly as Martin brought the boat to an even keel.

Pat found his eyes adjusting to the faint, luminous, blue illumination. It was the twilight of the hundred-fathom depth that had entranced Beebe in the first bathysphere descent, over a hundred years before. In this featureless blue void, now, the smallboat seemed to hang suspended. But Pat knew that they were rushing at high speed through the deep, a narrow beam of sonic vibration probing two miles in advance of them to herd sea creatures and drifting objects from their path.

Within only a few minutes they came upon a glittering, transparent wheel-shape with an open center. The blaze of its interior illumination extinguished by contrast the blue twilight. They were surrounded by darkness beyond the wheel.

Martin, slowing the smallboat, guided it up

through the center of the wheel-shape and through a magnetic iris into a docking pond. He slid back the transparent cover of the smallboat and both men stepped onto the side of the pond, into that clean, sea-smelling underwater atmosphere of the dwellings of their People.

"This way," said Martin, leading through a door. "The Sea Captains are all here. They've been waiting a couple of hours and the ones from the Pacific and Indian Oceans have to go clear around the world to get back to their areas. They all came."

Pat's eyebrows went up a little.

"All? To see me?" he said.

"Yes," said Martin, shortly, over his shoulder, and Pat followed the other man into a long conference room.

In the room he saw were a long table, chairs, a woman—and the tall Sea Captains. They were standing clustered at the far end of the table and they turned to look at Pat as he came in. Pat looked back with a sudden sense of shock.

He had become so used to the smaller people of the land that at first sight these, his own People, seemed to loom before him like giants in the clean-smelling room. It was not merely their height, which was like Pat's own, but the obvious power of their athletic, erect, and nearly naked bodies. Pat had forgotten. It was not here as it was on the land, where men ruled by mechanical device and social order, but by their own strengths and skills his People were lords of the sea.

Of the ten men and one woman now facing him, he knew perhaps four of the men by name from before his years of exile ashore. The ten were all of

his own third generation, who had sent their rep-
resentatives ashore at the request of Kai Ebberly,
sponsor of the Space Academy, to staff that in-
stitution of the land. Pat and they had been young
in the sea together.

They were young no longer. One to four years at
the Space Academy and six years since then of
being outlawed and hunted in the sea had brought
them to a scarred maturity. Their faces were grim
and hard. But, gazing at them narrowly, Pat saw
that in spite of the six years their eyes still glanced
level and straightforward. There was still none of
that shielded, dangerous subtlety in those eyes
against which Pat had learned to guard and ward,
in the eyes of the people ashore, among the
players of The Game.

Only the woman—the girl—had an unreadable
gaze. She was, Pat saw, third generation like all of
them, but perhaps half a dozen years younger.
Barely out of her teens.

"This," said Martin, introducing her, "is
Maytig Marieanna, Pat. She's our leading re-
searchist of the People, nowdays. —Let's sit
down."

Pat identified her then. She would be the
granddaughter of Anna Marieanna, the woman
scientist of the first-generation sea-born of the
People, who had first begun the study of the
changes that sea-birth was producing in those
who had given up the shore. Anna Marieanna had
been known as the most beautiful of her
generation—even after she had lost one arm and
been scarred in a shark attack. This girl had no
such beauty—but there was something about her,
nonetheless.

She was tawny-haired and tall; and her eyes

were blue, but chill as a storm sea. Yet for all that, along the channel of Pat's sea-senses, even dulled by the years ashore, came a sense of something singing in her that pulled hard upon him. —But Pat's own heart was in the keeping of a dark, slim woman ashore; and he made that dark image a successful shield against the singing.

They had seated themselves at the long table. Pat at one end, with Martin on his right and Maytig Marieanna on his left. He saw now that they were all silent, waiting for him to begin.

"Well," he said, looking around the table, "I suppose you want to know the answer to the message you sent ashore for me to pass on to Kai Ebberly? Here it is—Ebberly's ready to talk to a representative from the sea at any time—in fact, he says he'd have contacted you before this if he'd known how to go about it."

—As he said this, the brindle-haired, strong-jawed face of the Transportation Baron, middle-aged and harshly arrogant, rose in Pat's mind. They had talked for two hours the day before at Entertainment Estates North. Or rather—Ebberly had talked, charging Pat over and over again with a message to the People; and Pat had listened, reserving judgement in terms of his own private, separate committment.

". . . I don't suppose," Pat said now, "you want to tell me what you want to talk to him about?"

"Of course," said Maytig. For all the singing quality, there was something desperate and locked within her. "We want to come to terms with the land. This Hunting can't be allowed to go on any longer."

Pat nodded, bleakly.

"It's very bad, then?" he said.

"Over three thousand killed in the last eight months!" broke in Martin, savagely. He put his long hands on the table, leaning forward. "Three thousand lives—men, women, and children—for the perverted pleasure of any psychotic of the Land rich enough to buy a Hunter ship and equip it. By God, they don't hunt animals ashore like that, anymore, without a season and protection part of the time!"

Pat turned to look into Martin's face.

"Three thousand?" he said. "Out of three million of the People? You could pay a higher price. —And how many Hunters did you get?"

Martin's powerful fingers curled into half-fists. His lips thinned and a smile that was not humorous touched the grim corners of his mouth.

"Some hundreds . . ." he answered. "But not enough."

"—At any rate," said Maytig, drawing Pat's gaze back upon her, "that's not the point. The sea-children of the fourth generation aren't developing properly. They're showing hardly any, if any at all, increase in instincts and perceptions over our own third generation. This hiding in the depths is no good for them. They need the sunlight of the surface and the shallow coastal waters to develop properly. —And the years of their growing are fast slipping away from us. We've got to stop the Hunting and give them what they need."

"Ebberly," said Pat, bleakly, "sent me with a message. He'll save you from the Hunting and the outlawry at a price. He'll give you terms."

Maytig's stormy blue eyes flickered suddenly

and fiercely, as lightning flickers over a dark and heaving sea.

"That's not why we sent you a message to contact him for us," she answered. "We're not interested in his price. We'll give *him* terms. And he'll agree to them—unless he wants war."

"War?" Pat stared at her. "War between the People and the Land? There's three billion of them ashore and a world full of weapons and resources. Have you all lost your senses?"

Maytig's eyes hooded.

"There's a way," she said, flatly. "But we're not here to discuss that."

"No," said Pat, the bitterness creeping into his words in spite of himself, "you wouldn't want to tell me what it was."

Maytig shook her head at him, almost angrily.

"Don't talk like a fool, Patrick Joya!" she said. "Are we to judge a man by his actions, instead of what we read in him with our senses? Whatever your reason for taking the side of the shore, six years ago, there's no one in this room who doesn't feel you belong to the People and the Sea. —Do you feel you don't?"

"No," Pat shook his head. "I belong to the People and the Sea."

"Then let's forget the past," said Maytig. "The present is what's important. One of us has to go ashore to give our terms to Ebberly. And there's only one of us who's built for the job—as well as only one Ebberly will believe; because Ebberly knows how much Johnny means to the People."

"Johnny?" Pat looked at her in surprise. "But I heard—"

"You heard he'd left the People, taking his son

away after the bombing of the Castle-Homes,"
said Maytig. "That's right. But he'll come back
and lead us—if you ask him in the name of the
People."

"I?" Pat had reached the limits of his astonishment.

"That's Maytig's field," put in Martin. "She
knows more about the People than any of us. If she
says Johnny will listen to you, he will."

"It's simple enough, Pat," said Maytig. "The
same instincts that make us follow Johnny as our
natural leader, make it impossible for him to re-
fuse to lead us—if he knows the People really
need and want him as a whole. You, speaking for
the People, will prove that to him." She paused.
"Well, will you go ask him for us?"

Pat hesitated. He looked around all the faces at
the table and saw them all waiting.

"You know I can't say no," he answered at last.

"No," agreed Maytig gently. "You can't say
no—any more than Johnny can." She stood up,
looking around at the Sea Captains. "I'm satisfied,
if the rest of you are," she said.

Pat also rose.

"Someone will have to show me how to find
Johnny," he said.

"I'll take you," Maytig answered. "He's down
in the pack ice off the Ross Shelf Ice in the Antarctic. I've got my smallboat here, and it's a four-
seater. There'll be room for us to bring him and the
boy out."

Her certainty that Johnny would come made Pat
narrow his eyes at her. But the Captains were
standing up now. The meeting broke up swiftly.
Ten minutes later, Pat was back in a smallboat

with Maytig, and headed southeast on a course that would take them, some thousands of miles later, between Fernando da Noronha and Rocas Island, off Natal and the eastward bulge of South American Brazil.

The direct route—the shortest route—to the Ross Dependency and the Ross Shelf Ice, off the western curve of Antarctica between Victoria Land and Ellsworth Land, would have been south and southwest between Cuba and Haiti and so through the Panama or the Puerto Mexico Canals to the Pacific Ocean and then straight south. But those Canals were two parts of the world's seaways that not even an individual swimmer of the sea-People could sneak through. Pat and Maytig traveled through the twilight zone of the hundred-fathom depth with always a mile or more of water under their keel. Even at the two hundred knot speed, it was more than five days and nights before they approached the pack ice where Johnny and his son were known to be; and Pat, after six years away from the sea, in spite of his sea-birth was cramped and weary of the small space that was the smallboat's cockpit space.

There was only one incident on the long trip—and that came as they broke past Cape Horn, out of Drake's Passage into southern Pacific Ocean waters. A vague uncomfortableness had been nagging absently at Pat for some little time, like a toothache just below the level of attention, when Maytig turned abruptly about in the front cockpit and looked squarely at Pat.

"Feel anything?" she demanded. "I think someone's after us."

Pat stared for a second, then nodded.

"I've been feeling something for a little while,"
he said. "I just didn't identify it."

"Let's go up," said Maytig. She turned to touch
the controls before her and the little smallboat
pivoted its nose upward and stood on its jets. The
water lightened around them with startling rapid-
ity, and as Maytig touched the controls again,
deceleration hauled them forward in their seats.
Maytig slowed the smallboat to a drift and gradually at last brought it up to where the transparent
hood barely broke the surface of a wave.

They examined the empty ocean and sky as the
wave lifted them to its crest, and for a moment
Maytig brought the hood all the way out of the
water. There was nothing to be seen but the gray
and rolling surface of the sea under an icy blue
sky, that fitted like a steel helmet over the waves
around the circle of the horizon.

"All right," said Maytig. "We'll go deep."

She touched the controls. The smallboat nosed
over and plunged. It drove downward to the
twilight zone and through it in a vertical plunge.
It did not hesitate until both of them with their
third-generation senses, reinforcing the instruments of the smallboat, which had been designed
for all the generations of the sea-People, felt the
sea bottom approaching. Then Maytig slowed the
dive. They went down gently, and the smallboat
buried itself in the silt of radiolarian ooze at more
than a two mile depth. In the darkness and stillness, lit only by the small red instrument lights
from the control panels in front of them, they sat,
waiting and feeling.

Ten, fifteen . . . twenty minutes went by.

"All clear, I think," said Maytig at last. "How about you?"

"I haven't felt anything for nearly ten minutes," said Pat. "But I'm insensitive to the sea-feel and out of touch from being ashore so long. I was waiting for you to say something."

"Let's go, then," said Maytig. She touched the controls and the smallboat broke upwards from the ooze toward the twilight zone, leveled off and headed onward.

Ten hours later, they approached the surface and a huge floating piece of pan ice.

"Someone's coming to meet us," said Maytig, slowing the smallboat to a stop as they glided in by the vast underwater shadow of the chunk of pan ice.

"Johnny?" asked Pat, envying her undulled sea-senses.

"I don't think so—" she broke off suddenly. A dark shadow twice the length of the smallboat had materialized out of the dimness and resolved itself into a bull killer whale. The dark, intelligent eye, and the permanently grinning mouth slid by a foot or two from the transparent hood of the smallboat, looking in at them. Pat reached instinctively for the sonic rifle clipped to the side of his cockpit. "—No, it's all right," said Maytig. "That'll be the killer whale that belongs to Johnny's boy. We've heard about it."

"Belongs?" Pat stared out through the transparent canopy at the huge and murderous shape of the cetacean. "You can't make a pet or a sea-friend of a wild killer."

"Tomi Joya has. —Here he is now," Maytig

interrupted herself as a boyish figure in black, coldwater skins showed up alongside the canopy and waved asking to be let into the smallboat. She slid back a section of the canopy and the boy slipped through the magnetic envelope to drop wetly to the air-filled seat of the rear cockpit alongside Pat, shoving back a face mask as he did so.

"I'm Tomi Joya—I remember you, Pat," he said, with the directness of the People. He looked forward at Maytig, who was turned about in her cockpit to face them. "I don't think I remember you, though."

"Maytig Marieanna," said Maytig. "Where's Johnny—your father?"

"In the berg-Home. I'll show you," said Tomi. "You go down under the ice. Then we'll have to leave the smallboat and swim up the tunnel." He looked back at Pat. "You came for my dad at last. That's good."

"Oh?" said Pat. "How do you know what we've come for? And why should it be good?" He spoke more gruffly than he meant. Tomi could not be expected to know how he resembled his father— as Pat remembered Johnny from their own boyhoods in the sea together.

"You wouldn't have come, except to get him," said the boy, with a strangely adult calmness and certainty. "And it's good because it's time. He's been sitting here too long."

He turned to Maytig, studying her for a moment. To Pat's interested observation, there was a powerful, almost brutal quality of penetration in the search of the boy's eyes—as if he could see into Maytig's very soul. And Maytig reacted curi-

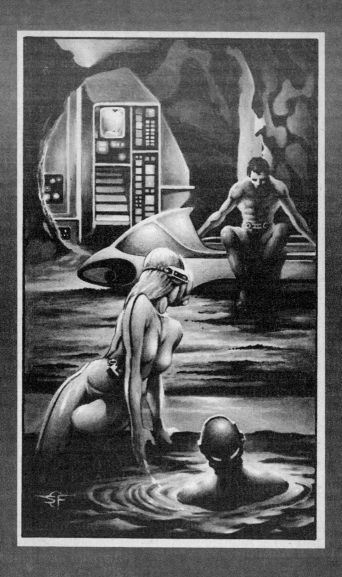

ously, stiffening and lifting her chin slightly as if in defiance of the examination.

"Take this smallboat down under the berg-chunk," Tomi said, finally. "I'll show you where our tunnel is."

Maytig turned and touched the controls before her. The smallboat slid down under the berg. Tomi directed them to the tunnel entrance and a moment later, leaving the smallboat behind, the three of them rose up the tunnel into the berg-Home.

They hauled themselves from the pool and turned toward the unmoving, dark figure seated before them on the shadowy form of a sea-sled. Tomi went to the power unit and touched it.

Light burst on suddenly, whitely and powerfully flooding the ice-brilliant interior of the berg-Home.

The seated figure raised its head. Johnny smiled up at the visitors and got to his feet.

"Hello, Pat," he said, as if the six years since they had seen each other had been no time at all. But then his gaze went past Pat to Maytig and the smile faded.

"Hello, Johnny," Pat was answering. But Johnny did not hear him. Johnny's gaze was locked with the gaze of Maytig; and—as simply as that—he discovered the first uncharted reef of his calculated course plainly before him.

Rare among the sense-dulled people of the land, but common in the sea, where instincts had been reawakened and sharpened, was the soundless shock of a common identity felt between man and woman at first sight. Johnny had felt it himself once before—with Sarah Light, Tomi's mother. He had never expected to feel it again. But here it was; and he saw by Maytig's eyes that she had felt it, also.

Therefore, the hidden reef that threatened his plans. For if he should take the leadership of the People which he knew these two had come to offer him, the time might come when the instinct of that leadership might come in conflict with the instinct that would lead him from this moment on to keep and protect Maytig.

He woke to the fact that Pat was frowning at him—that Pat had seen his reaction to Maytig and understood it. Johnny opened his mouth to say something; what, he did not know—

But at the moment Baldur, the dolphin, exploded upward out of the water in the ice-pool of the berg-Home, crying out excitedly in the high-pitched twittering of the dolphin people. All four of the sea-born in the room spun to face him—but it was the boy, Tomi, who translated first.

"Something coming!" he shouted. "Something coming, fast, with a fix on us here. Like a smallboat, only bigger—and with a Lander wake! A Hunter! A *Hunter!*"

# 5

Johnny moved at once, snatching up his cold-water skins and mask from the sea-sled. But by the time he had them on, the other three were already gone under the surface of the ice-pool and out of sight. He dived after them and plunged down through the ice tunnel toward the open sea.

He emerged between Pat and Maytig with Tomi a little space off, each apart and facing outwards in the direction of the open sea underwater. The dolphin Baldur and Conquistador, the killer whale, loomed in the green dimness nearby. Johnny turned toward the open sea himself and let himself hang in the water.

For a moment he felt nothing. Impatiently, he jerked open the faceplate of his mask, so that the cold water rushed icily against the skin of his face and his vision blurred. Now he could see nothing;

he was as blind as any Lander, underwater. But—clearly now, racing to his third-generation senses, came the faint, indefinable sensation against the skin of his face that was the advance vibration of the shock wave made by some swiftly approaching, hard, unnatural object parting the underwater under its own power. The sensation was leaping at him at the near mile-a-second underwater speed of sound; and it was proof positive that some man-made object was approaching. No living creature of the sea produced such a shock wave as it traveled through the water. And not even the sea-People had succeeded in designing an underwater craft that did not.

As Tomi had said, this craft approaching, judging by the size of its shock wave, must be about the proportions of a small-Home. Though it was possible it was much smaller, and the size of its shock wave due to crude Lander design and building.

Johnny replaced his faceplate and blew its interior clear of the seawater he had trapped in it. He looked around at the others.

"We were followed, all right," said Maytig to Pat.

But she did not speak the words aloud. She made them instead in the clicking code which utilized tongue and fingernails, known to the People as the dolphin code. Maytig turned toward Johnny; and Johnny saw the girl's face dimly through the thicknesses of their two faceplates and the foot or so of water that separated them.

"It's a Hunter all right," clicked Maytig, tensely. "Johnny, take my smallboat and run for it. With only one man's weight inside, it'll be able to outrun the Hunter. The rest of us will keep him busy here while you're getting away."

Johnny stared at her without moving.

"What are you waiting for?" coded Maytig. "You owe your life to the People! They need you. They can get along without the rest of us if they have to, but there's only one of you. Get going!"

"She's right, Johnny," clicked Pat. "The rest of us aren't important. If it's Tomi you're worried about, he can keep his killer whale between him and the Hunter ship and they'll probably never suspect he's here. But it'll take both Maytig and me to hold the Hunter ship up, while you're getting away."

"Hurry!" messaged Maytig, impatiently. "It'll be here in a minute or two. Can't you feel it coming?"

"Never mind that," coded Johnny. He looked through the water at both of them. "Is this what the People do now, when one of these ships corners them? Just run—or give up and die?"

"What else do you expect them—or us—to do?" demanded Maytig, angrily. "Sonic rifles won't hurt the Hunters inside a hull body of even quarter-inch metal. And they're using magnetic envelopes just like ours now around their ships, so they can follow us right down to bottom pressures, no matter how deep we try to hide. They've got sonic cannon mounted outside their ships so they can shoot us without exposing themselves. Why do you think we've been living a hundred fathoms deep all these years? The only way the People can fight them is by massing enough small-Homes around them so that men with cutting torches can open their hulls and let the sea in!"

"And there're only two of us. Get going, Johnny," said Pat. "While there's still time."

Johnny shook his head. Something— a protective instinct directed toward any of the sea-People—that had been dormant in him since he had seen Tomi's mother dead, had been awakened again whether he wanted it or not. And this element in him stood still to see that Maytig and Pat were so embedded in the structure of things as they were that they could not imagine trying to change it. Johnny felt the sense of command, the old clear-headedness and certainty of decision flooding back in to him like a remembered skill. He turned to Maytig.

"It's hull's metal and only one quarter of an inch thick, you say?" he coded.

"Quarter inch magnesium alloy, that's all," Maytig answered. "I told you, they depend on the magnetic envelopes for pressure protection now, just as we do. Why do you think they're fast enough nowadays to run our small-Homes down when they catch them in open water?"

"All right," said Johnny in the code. He turned to his son. "Tomi, take Conquistador back behind the bulge of the bottom of the ice here, and when I call for him, send him in to help me. But don't come yourself—understand? You're to get in the smallboat with Pat and Maytig and do what they say."

He turned to the others.

"You two take the smallboat back with Tomi and Conquistador. And stay out of sight unless you have to make a run for it."

The difference in his coding, in his manner, checked whatever protest Maytig was about to make. The girl hung as if undecided in the water.

"What about you? What are you going to do?" asked Pat.

"Fight," said Johnny.

"You can't!" coded Maytig, sharply. "I tell you—"

"Then I'll fight with you," coded Pat, calmly. "Maytig and Tomi can get away faster in the smallboat without my extra weight if they have to run for it."

"If!" said Maytig. She looked desperately at Johnny. "I'm going to stick with you too! Tomi can drive a smallboat, can't he?"

"He knows how," said Johnny. "All right, you two stay with me, if you want to. Tomi, take the smallboat and your killer back out of sight."

Tomi tumbled into the smallboat and broke it loose from its magnetic mooring alongside the tunnel mouth. Boat and boy and killer whale vanished away behind the downward hanging bulge of the underside of the berg-chunk.

Johnny looked back at the other two and saw that sonic rifles were already in their hands. They must have taken them from the smallboat before he had time to join them.

"Pat," he said, "give me your weapon. You'll find another rifle up in the berg-Home beside the power unit." Pat handed over the gun he was carrying, turned, and shot up the tunnel, leaving Maytig and Johnny face to face.

"We can bolt up the tunnel, if we have to," said Johnny.

"And be trapped," coded Maytig. "Do you want to wait out here for them?"

Pat came back down the tunnel, carrying Johnny's sonic rifle.

"I want them to be sure to see me," said Johnny. "As soon as they show up you and Pat jump up the tunnel. Can they tell how many of us there are, under the ice?"

"They use instruments, not instincts," said Maytig, "but they can tell there are three of us here all right—" She broke off abruptly; and she and Pat kicked powerfully toward the tunnel as Johnny twitched about in the water. There had been no need for further warnings. The sudden shock of the Hunter ship's change of course toward the underside of the berg had been message enough.

Maytig vanished up the tunnel with Pat right behind her. Johnny hung still at the entrance. All the dullness and introspection of the last six years were gone from him now. He felt cool and alert, waiting actually to see the Hunter.

He held his position until the Lander vessel literally swung into sight around the bottom curve of the ice from the seaward side of the chunk. It braked with its front jets to a hard-shocked halt, facing him and less than twenty feet away through the water. From behind its cabin window, above the control chairs, two faces stared at him in astonishment—a lean face, and a round one with a heavy, brown mustache.

He looked back. The ship, he saw, was squat, bulbous, and red, with the yellow plumb bob emblem of the Construction Group on its side—

though this meant little or nothing. Even Johnny
had heard, in his rare contacts with the sea-People
during the six years, that world opinion was
enough against Hunting so that those who hunted
often used false names and emblems. All this observation of his, though it actually took place in
only the shortest of moments, seemed to be done
leisurely by Johnny. He glanced back at the faces
staring at him through the cabin windshield of
the Hunter and found them still fixed as if by a
spell.

Strangely, he had no doubt that he could move
before they could come to life and threaten him.
Once, on leave from the Space Academy ashore,
he had gone to see a bullfight in Mexico City. In
the bullfight the moment had come when the bull,
baffled by the swirling cape in the slim, brown
hands of the matador, had stopped dead in his
tracks and the matador had turned his back on the
animal and walked slowly away toward the protective barrier behind him. While the bull stood
still, baffled, saliva dripping from its black muzzle, the man had walked slowly toward Johnny,
and under the tricorn hat of the matador Johnny
had seen a faint frown, as of thoughtful concentration, a look of fine-sharpened professional certainty.

Now, Johnny felt a parallel certainty in himself.
The two Hunters sat as if frozen in a dream, staring at this sea-outlaw who did not try to escape,
but faced them calmly. Deliberately, unexcitedly,
Johnny turned his head and called through his
mask diaphragm in spoken words.

"Tomi!" he called. "—Now!"

At the same time he turned and shot up the
water-filled tunnel. He was almost to the pool in

the berg-Home when the shock of the blow from the Hunter's sonic cannon striking the tunnel mouth washed up after him through the tunnel, baffled but not completely absorbed by the berg-ice. A fraction of a second later came the shock of a different impact against the underside of the ice and there was the high-pitched, water-born crunching of crushed and battered metal.

Reaching the open pool where there was room to turn, Johnny flipped over and dived back down the tunnel, feeling Pat and Maytig close behind him. As they reached open water under the ice, another metal-bending impact jarred and sounded around them and they tumbled out into the undersea to see Tomi, with gesture and voice, commanding his now blood-mad killer whale back from a third attack on the Hunter ship.

Crushed and flooding with icy water, the red vessel, turning up the yellow compass and bob painted on one side of her, was falling away into the mile-deep ocean like a wounded bird struck by a hawk. The single magnetic envelope that would have protected her, by deflecting the inanimate pressure of the deep even six miles down, had given way, as it was designed to do, against the imbalance of pressure against one small area of it. Pressure such as a single entering swimmer might exert—or the living battering ram of a thirty-five-foot long killer whale ramming with the speed of a dolphin—and capable of driving up through six feet of rotten sea ice to get at a basking seal.

Now the Hunter ship was fluttering down out of sight. And the two men inside her were drowning or already dead. There was no hope of saving them even if they deserved saving. Tomi, Pat, and

Maytig drifted close to Johnny in the water, and together they watched the wreckage dwindling until it faded from sight in the darkness of the green depths and was gone.

Johnny watched it disappear with a cold, conclusive feeling. For six years he had heard about these Hunters, psychotics of the Land who had made a sport of chasing and killing the outlawed People of the sea; but this was the first time he had met two of them face to face.

However that had been his intention. It was the reason he had lingered below the tunnel as they had come up and stopped in the water. He had seen what he had suspected he might see. The Hunters had not been here by chance. They had somehow followed Maytig's smallboat purposely to the berg-Home; and they had known they were after Johnny Joya.

That was why it had seemed to them too good to be true when they had suddenly come upon the man they were seeking, waiting for them. It had smelled of some kind of trap—and that was why they had simply sat staring at him, frozen in indecision; while Conquistador, unseen, drove in on them from beneath the low-hanging belly of the berg-ice.

They had been sent from somewhere ashore with a mission to kill him, Johnny. There was only one plainly obvious suspect who might have been able to dispatch such a mission—and that was Kai Ebberly, who knew the Sea Captains would be contacting their former leader. But Ebberly, who knew how necessary Johnny was to any negotiations between himself and the sea-People, would hardly have sent assassins to kill the one man with whom he could best talk.

From the analog, Johnny had deduced plainly that Ebberly, prime mover and greatest of the Barons, was almost certainly controller of one of the two fuses to Armageddon that sputtered ashore. The identity of whoever controlled the other, however, had been unreadable—a shadow within the maze of the analog.

Deliberately now, Johnny tried to summon up the image of that shadowy other, once again. But already his involvement in events concerned with the analog had distorted and blurred his ability to read from it. He would have to find the identity of the other by more direct, different means—unless the other chose to reveal himself by approaching Johnny first, which was strongly unlikely.

Events would shape the situation; and from that shape as it emerged he would have to plot his actions. —There remained the business on which Maytig and Pat had come to see him. He knew what that business was, but for the present he dared not reveal the extent of his analog-won knowledge to anyone.

Least of all to Maytig—under the shadow of the sudden emotional bond that had sprung into existence between them. For now he had laid his hand to the wheel and could not turn back. And it might be that events would require that he be ruthless—even with her—to save both land and sea. Therefore, he must go through the motions, now, of not knowing the *why* of their coming.

He turned to Maytig and Pat.

"You came here for some reason," he said.

"Ebberly wants to negotiate with the People,"

said Pat. "And the People want you to speak for them with him. —I came to urge you to do it, too." His face plate glanced toward Tomi, still holding to the wickedly high back fin of Conquistador. "They can care for Tomi for you, while you're ashore."

"That's all right," said Johnny. "It's time he met his own people again, anyway."

"Then you'll come?" said Maytig, almost sharply. He looked at her.

"Didn't you know I would?" he asked.

"Yes," she said. In the shadow of her mask, her face looked strange. "But knowing it—and now, knowing you—are two different things.

# 6

They sank the sea-sled and the power equipment to the bottom under the pack ice and cached it there with a marker. They filled the four-seater smallboat, and headed west and north toward the waters between the Coral and Tasman Seas, where Maytig's sea-lab was in movement, east of the Great Barrier Reef off Australia's west coast.

Conquistador and Baldur were left to follow at their own speed. It would take them a little while, but their sea-senses for direction and location, which even the first sea-born generation of the People had come to share, would bring the killer and dolphin finally to Tomi at the sea-lab which the two cetaceans had never seen.

Meanwhile, the smallboat with its four human passengers arrived at the sea-lab and arrangements were immediately made to send Pat ashore near Sydney at Entertainment Estates South, where he could make arrangements for Johnny's interview with Kai Ebberly.

The sea-lab was composed of two ring-shaped Homes fastened magnetically one above the other. It housed a staff of more than twenty people and kept four of these in two-seater smallboats always on patrol in the surrounding waters to warn and protect the lab against Hunter ships from the land. Right now it was in movement to the northwest to keep up with the hunting movement on the lightless ocean bottom, two miles below, of one of the giant, deep-sea cephalopods that resembled a monster squid. It was the reactions of this sea-creature that the lab was currently studying. To Johnny, watching with Tomi and Maytig as the people of the lab got ready a smallboat and a pilot to deliver Pat ashore in Australia, it was strangely interesting to see the respect the sea-lab staff gave Maytig. It was more than respect. It was a sort of a tenderness, not unmixed with awe, for this girl who was younger than most of them.

"Someone from the land will meet you offshore from Savannah Stand," said Pat to Johnny, as the lean man prepared to step down into his seat in the smallboat that would take him ashore. "I don't know the details, but I know the general way Ebberly wants to work it. You'll be met with clothes and a credit card and taken in to the Terminal. From there, you'll take the subway to Transportation Estates North near Land O'Lakes, Wisconsin. I'll meet you at the Estates entrance and take you on inside. Ebberly's planned a dinner for the Barons and I'll have come in with Mila

Jhan, the Entertainment Baroness, to attend.
You'll leave with us in the Entertainment private
rocket for Australia, after it's over. Got it?"

"Got it," said Johnny. He and Pat looked at each
other for a moment, feeling the old closeness they
had known as boys building once more between
them, then Pat stepped down into the smallboat,
the cover closed over his head, and the smallboat
slid through the magnetic pressure iris of the
parking pond to vanish in the twilit depths of the
underseas a hundred fathoms deep.

"Come along to my office, Johnny," said Maytig
putting her hand on his arm. "I'd like to talk to
you." She turned to the boy. "Tomi—you can find
something to amuse yourself with, can't you?"

"I'm going to look around up near the surface,"
said Tomi. "The water feels different here. I want
to know something about it when Baldur and
Conquistador get here. They'll be coming in day
after tomorrow."

"They can't get here that soon," said Maytig.

"Day after tomorrow," said the boy positively.
His head moved slightly as if he was looking and
listening to something outside the sea-lab. "They
can go faster than you think when they really
want to. They'll be tired when they get here."

He turned and went over to the lockers nearby
to get himself a waterlung and a sonic rifle.
Maytig led Johnny away through the sea-lab and
into a section of it furnished as a small office.

"I want you to see some films," said Maytig,
once they were seated. She clipped a spool into
the unit on her desk and the desktop suddenly
dissolved into a three-dimensional scene showing the interior of a small-Home of the People.

This particular small-Home was inhabited by a third-generation mother and father, a grandmother of the second generation, and a fourth-generation boy somewhat smaller than Tomi. The small-Home moved through the hundred fathom depth, occasionally venturing to the surface for a few cautious moments, occasionally diving to deep sea-bottom to hide in the radiolarian ooze from signal of Hunters of the Land. The routine of their life seemed calm enough, although the faces of the family—even that of the boy under its shock of black hair—were less smiling than had once been the habit of the People.

Yet, Johnny's gaze came to concentrate more and more on the boy. Slowly, he stiffened in his chair.

"How old's that boy?" he demanded at last.

"Six months younger than Tomi," answered Maytig, from the other side of the desk. Johnny lifted his head to look at her.

"I see," he said, simply.

"I thought you would," replied Maytig. She shut off the unit, and the picture vanished from the desktop between them. She looked up to meet the gaze of Johnny.

"You see how he is," she said, "barely six months younger than Tomi and hardly advanced, at all, over his third-generation parents in any way. While Tomi's away advanced, in growth and instincts both, over any of us of the third. Granted he's the oldest of his fourth generation. Granted—he's your son. But the real reason for his difference is the fact that he's been able to grow up free, near the surface, without fear or restraint. The others haven't —and the time's run out when they can wait any longer for what Tomi's been able to take for granted."

"That's what you want me to tell Ebberly?" Johnny said.

"If you think best," she said. "Tell him we have to have the shallow waters and the surface of the seas—even if we have to kill the Land to get them."

"Kill the Land?" In spite of the knowledge he had gained from the analog, Johnny chilled. Here it was, then—the fuse in the sea he had read from the mental counterpart of the land-sea forces.

"Yes," said Maytig. She touched the unit on her desk again, and a map sprang into being on the desktop. A map of the world—but on it all sea and land were different shapes. Johnny bent close, frowning, staring at it. There was something familiar about the way a greatly increased Mediterranean swelled vastly into what were now the land masses of Africa, Europe, and Asia. He pointed to it.

"Why, that's the Tethys sea," he said, "the way it was in the Permian Period of the Paleozoic, a couple of million years ago."

"No," said Maytig, and her voice was so different suddenly that he looked sharply at her. "That's the way the world will look if the Land forces us to fight them for survival." She drew a deep breath. "You've heard of the Ring of Fire?"

"The ring of volcanic areas encircling the main areas of the Pacific Ocean basin?" Johnny asked.

She nodded.

"We've suspected for some time that there were certain trigger points, at certain spots below the sea-bottom itself, on the Mohorovicic Discontinuity where the earth's mantle touches the crustal covering above. —Trigger points on which the present crustal balance depends. In the last few years we've found these trigger points—or enough of them to take action. We've bored to them and planted nuclear explosives."

She stopped, and looked at him as if asking him to complete the message for her—so that she would not have to put it into words herself. But Johnny sat silent, watching her.

"If we fire those charges," she said, looking squarely at him, "that crustal balance will be upset. And the result will be—" She pointed at the table top. She took another deep breath. "Well, you understand. If we fire those charges, cushioned here in the middle of the deep sea, far from land, we of the People can ride out the changes without harm. But most of the present continental dry land areas will be sunk—and flood, earthquake, fire, and storm will destroy most ashore of what's left."

She sat back in her chair with the weary settling of one who has passed off a heavy load onto the shoulders of another.

"There it is, Johnny," she said. "For five years I've been the watchdog of the fourth generation. It's been up to me to say how much more of this unnatural living they could take before losing their birthright of improved senses over us of the third. Because"—she eyed him carefully—"the total change occurring in us of the sea is an evolutionary change, Johnny. That's what the work begun by my grandmother has ended up showing us. Ashore, evolution of man had stopped. But our coming back to the sea started it again after hundreds of thousands of years. It's not just for the sea-People we'd have the right to destroy the Land, Johnny. It's for the future of the human race."

She paused. Her voice changed.

"It's been up to me to give the order to kill the Land, Johnny," she said. "But you're back now. It's up to you."

She was looking at him, suddenly differently again, her eyes tragic that she must put this load on him, whom she had abruptly discovered she loved. While Johnny, himself, looked back, being careful to keep his own eyes unreadable.

For this was the fuse in the sea, whose existence he had read in the analog. And it was as he had feared, from the first sight of Maytig in the berg-Home.

Maytig and the fuse were interlinked. She, with Ebberly and the shadowy Other, ashore, and the yet-undiscovered fuse-holder that was somehow *in sea on land* were all four those against whom Johnny must work. And as he might have to destroy Ebberly—or any of the others—that the Land and Sea might live; so might he have to destroy her who looked at him now with love and sympathy in her eyes.

So ran the present path of his calculations across that bleak ocean of the chartless future.

# 7

Pat was waiting for him in the lobby, when, just at sunset, he reached Transportation Estates North Land O'Lakes on the Wisconsin-Michigan border. The Estates Terminal was as large as the public terminal of a small city. Pat led the way to the end of the Terminal Building and they came to a wide portal at which were Baron's Men in blue and white Transportation livery, carrying not only belt weapons but sonic rifles. Pat showed these a pair of passes and he and Johnny were waved through.

They emerged into a park-like area and took one of several moving walkways, which carried them off through the trees at a speed close to fifteen miles an hour.

"It's a large place," said Pat, noticing Johnny's eyebrows raise as the walkway accelerated up to its terminal speed. "About fifteen by twenty miles."

Johnny nodded.

The walkway was carrying them now beneath trees toward a lake on the edge of which was a white, single-story pavilion surrounded by leaf-shrouded arbors that also enclosed a wide, raised platform facing the lake.

Men in livery were serving food and drink there to people occupying half the chairs around a horseshoe-shaped banquet table, white-tableclothed, furnished with silver, china, and glassware, all of an antique pattern. These furnishings, the platform, and the people themselves, who moved or sat and chattered, were bathed not only in the concealed lighting from the arbors on three sides surrounding, but by the last autumnal light of the slow-setting northern sun, now descending into the far waters of the lake. In that last sunlight, the white cloth of the table was reddened and stained.

Then, the walkway carried Pat and Johnny on past, in through an entrance arbor covered with the crooked leaves of Dutchman's-pipe, and into the interior of the pavilion itself. It stopped at last in a hallway where a white-haired elderly man in white slacks and shirt met them.

"I'm Patrick Joya," said Pat, to this man. The white head bent in something between a bow and a nod.

"This way," said the elderly man. He led them through several rooms and into a wide, low-ceilinged room, part sitting room, part office. In front of a wide balcony opening on the lake itself was a desk. But the rest of the floor was covered with lounging chairs and armchairs.

"Wait here," said the man. He left the room. Pat walked almost to the desk and chose a chair. Johnny sat down in a neighboring one.

"You've met Kai Ebberly?" asked Pat. Johnny nodded.

"When he used to visit the Space Academy," he said. "Several times. I was Cadet Colonel. Remember?"

"I remember," said Pat. "It doesn't seem that long ago somehow—" He turned, and Johnny with him, to see two men entering the room.

One, Johnny recognized immediately as Ebberly. The other, a shorter, oddly wide-shouldered figure, he identified a little belatedly as Barth Stuve, who had become Baron of Construction only shortly before the sea-Cadets had left the Space Academy, six years before. Even as he recognized the man, Johnny became aware that Barth's eyes had glanced across the room to focus on him with a strange, dark intensity.

"Oh, you two?" said Ebberly, stopping abruptly, and with no noticeable change in tone. "I'd almost forgotten about your business. —I want to talk to these men, privately. See you shortly at the banquet, Barth."

It was a simple statement, but uttered in a tone of almost royal command. With another, fleeting, glance at Johnny, Barth murmured something, turned, and went.

Ebberly came on alone, setting one foot directly before the other—a blocky, reddish-haired man in his late forties, with thick, blunt-boned hands and

a square face. It had been common knowledge,
Johnny remembered, that when Ebberly gave way
to anger the heavy-colored flushing of his face
made the freckles stand out as light, rather than
dark, spots on the leathery skin. In that face now,
his eyes were a bright, opaque blue, like bits of
colored chinaware, below thick, straw-colored
eyebrows and above a strong nose and spade-
shaped chin. He strode up to Johnny and Pat,
dropped into a chair and snapped his fingers. A
man in white appeared.

"Sit down," said Ebberly to the two tall young
men. "What'll you drink?"

"Nothing," said Johnny, coldly, as they two sat
down. "Just get to the point. What've you got in
mind for us?"

Ebberly stared at him for a moment. Johnny let
him stare. Ebberly's face, molded and lined by
forty-eight years of power and a single, unvarying
character, could not cast itself into an expression
of bafflement. But his blue eyes seemed to shutter
uncertainly for the fraction of a second, as a turning plate reflects a beam of light for an instant. He
gave a short, harsh and ragged laugh and waved
the man in white out of the room.

"What I've got in mind for you—" he echoed.
For a second his face seemed uncertain. "Well,
I've got a suggestion." His voice regained its normal strength of tone. "It's more than a suggestion,
it's the one possible solution for you people. I
can't change the fact you've been outlawed by
decision of the Council of Barons. The rest of them
passed that over my objection in the first place.
But I'll make all your people safe for a price."

"A price?" said Johnny.

Ebberly stared hard-eyed at him. The Baron appeared once more in control of himself and the situation.

"You didn't think I'd pussyfoot around you and pretend it was anything but a price?" he said. "You know what I'm after. What I've been after from the first. The stars. A faster-than-light means of getting out beyond the solar system. It's what the world needs and I'm going to produce it. We were headed for it with our Space Bat research, when you took your sea-Cadets home from the Space Academy, six years back."

"And you couldn't find qualified volunteers—qualified Cadets—on land to replace us, could you?" said Johnny. "So the Academy's been closed down ever since. Isn't that right?"

"That's right!" Ebberly stared grimly at him. "I'm not trying to pretend you people from the sea don't have something to bargain with. The people on the land here have lost faith in getting out to the far stars. But it's not their fault. It's living piled on top of each other this way, playing their so-called Game of Life. Never mind that now. I need Space Cadets. You staff my Academy and get it working again and I'll guarantee that the days of your people's being hunted and outlawed will be over."

"How?" said Johnny. But he said it almost absently, watching the Transportation Baron as if the expression on Ebberly's face was more important than the answer.

"Come ashore. Come ashore in small parties to my Transportation Terminals and Stands. I'll have people waiting there for you to pin on the mark of our Group and make you members in it.

Once you're Transportation members no one in any other Group can say a word against you. That's how society's set up ashore here, now more than ever. The theory of Group protection of its individual members is something no one wants to threaten. No one's going to try to shake that."

"Are you sure?" asked Johnny, very softly. Once more, Ebberly stared at him for a long moment, and the china-blue eyes shuttered for a second.

"What do you mean?" he demanded, at last.

Johnny stood up.

"I mean," said Johnny, "that we'll think over your offer. —Even though a lot of the sea-People have died in the last six years, and even though I'm not so sure you didn't plan this whole scheme from the first, just to force us back to your Academy."

"By God!" Ebberly was on his feet. For a moment it looked as if he would throw himself at Johnny's throat in spite of their difference in size. Then, he checked, and the color faded again from his face. Johnny had not moved or changed expression. "All right. And maybe I was unconsciously thinking ahead to now, when I let them back me down in the Council on the motion to outlaw you sea-People six years ago. But I tell you this, Joya, I've never lied, and never needed to lie or break my word to anyone in my life. —If I was thinking ahead, I'm not ashamed of it. Because, in the end, when I get the human race out beyond the solar system at last—it'll have been worth it!"

He stared hard at Johnny a second more, then turned and walked swiftly to his desk.

"I'm going to the banquet now," he said over

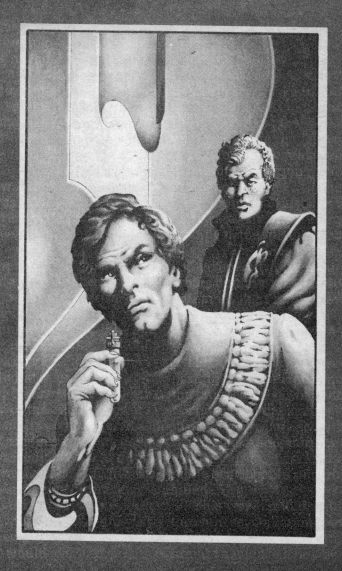

his shoulder to Pat. "Make sure he's stashed somewhere out of sight, Pat, before you show up yourself. —You know what to do." He opened the drawer of the desk, took out something, and tossed it to Johnny.

Johnny caught it in mid-air and looked at it. It was a capped, four-inch test tube three-quarters filled with a clear liquid. He took off the cap, and sniffed at the liquid.

"Sea-water," he said. "Shore water, Narragan-set Bay. —And what else?" He looked at Ebberly.

"Cost me fifty thousand to have a man steal me that sample," said Ebberly. "What else? A lab-produced, free-swimming, independent muta-tion of *salmonella* bacteria. There's enough in that tube to—in a hundred years—multiply, in-fect, poison, and kill-off everything warm-blooded that lives in the seas—including people. They used to think the seas were too big to be poisoned—not any more."

He slammed shut the desk drawer and came around the desk, headed toward the door.

"We've got some impatient elements ashore here," he said. "That's what I'm trying to save you people from. Don't take too much time making up your minds."

He went out. Johnny and Pat watched him swinging, heel-and-toe toward the room en-trance. And then he was through it and gone.

"Well," said Pat, slowly into the silence that followed. "At least he's got a reputation for keep-ing his word. If he says he'll take care of the sea-People once they're ashore, he'll do it." He looked curiously at Johnny. "His word is good."

"His word," said Johnny, grimly, still looking

at the now empty doorway, "isn't worth a plugged chip." He put the test tube in his pocket.

Pat's gaze tightened.

"What do you mean?" Pat said. "He's always kept his word. It's a reputation he's built up the world over."

"Exactly," said Johnny. "It's the reputation he values, not the word." He turned to meet the eyes of his cousin. "You aren't suggesting I take him at his word?"

"God forbid!" said Pat, violently. He opened his mouth as if to say something more, but checked himself. He turned away from Johnny's gaze. "I'll talk to you later. Come on. Right now I've got to find you a place to stay for the next forty-five minutes or so while I put in an appearance at the banquet."

He led the way out of the building and onto a different walkway. This carried them around the long, low shape of the pavilion and to the screen of leafy arbors through which Johnny could see the now brightly-lit banquet platform. They left the walkway for one of the arbors.

"You can wait safely here," Pat told Johnny, and pointed to the back of a slim, tall dark-haired girl seated at the near leg of the banquet table, facing the other way. "That's Mila Jhan, the head of the Entertainment Group. They'll be seating me close to her. You'll have me in sight all the time, and if any trouble comes up I can signal you. All right?"

"Fine," said Johnny. He watched Pat go off through the arbors and up to the platform, to be seated—as he had said—at a chair next to the Entertainment Group's woman leader. Johnny sat down himself in the shadow of the arbor, on one of the white chairs at the round, white table. His thoughts were just starting to drift back to Ebberly, when he heard a faint sound from the arbor entrance behind him. Swiftly, he turned.

There was a figure standing there. By a trick of the light coming through the arbor, the face of the figure was masked in anonymous shadow, but below this darkness the light from the platform cut squarely across the exaggerated shoulders of a fur jacket Johnny had seen earlier.

"Hello, Johnny Joya," said the soft voice of the man Johnny had identified as Barth Stuve.

"Pardon me?" said Johnny.

"Oh," said the nearly whispering voice of Stuve. "It wasn't hard to recognize you, even after six years, from your class pictures in the Space Academy Annual. I've been waiting for you to show up here. I've wanted to talk to you for a long time, Johnny."

The whisper rang more loudly upon Johnny's ears than had been intended. Up on the banquet platform a little silence had fallen. Up there, they were asking Pat to sing them something. Someone was handing him a guitar. Johnny smiled grimly through the darkness at Stuve. This man had somehow known Johnny was coming and had been here to meet him. It was plain enough, now. This man was the shadowy other in the analog—the second holder, ashore, of a fuse to Armageddon.

"If you wanted to talk to me," answered Johnny, "why did you send someone to kill me?"

Stuve chuckled in darkness.

"You figured that out?" he said. "I knew Pat

was going back to the sea on an errand for
Ebberly—that meant he'd come to you eventually.
It was just a matter of the last meal he ate ashore
having a harmless but heavy metallic salt added
to it—one that it would take his body about a week
to eliminate entirely—and he showed up bright
on the tracers of my Hunter ship."

"Which won't be coming back," said Johnny.

Stuve chuckled again.

"I never liked my Cousin Larry anway," he said.

Up on the platform, Pat struck the first few
chords on the guitar and began to sing.

> "—I met my mates in the morning and, oh,
> but I am old—"

Johnny's smile harshened in the private darkness. It was *Lukannon*, the song Pat was singing;
the seal-song Rudyard Kipling had written as a
poem nearly two hundred years ago—the anthem
of the hunted fur seals, set by Pat to music, that
was become the private anthem of the Hunted
sea-People. He was throwing it now in the Lander
faces, up there around the banquet tables, though
they did not realize that.

"—But you haven't answered me," said Johnny.
"Why send someone to kill me, if you wanted to
talk to me?"

"I had to make sure," murmured Stuve, under
Pat's singing. "After six years you might not have
been the same man any more."

"The same man?" said Johnny. "Why bother to
check on that?"

"Because . . ." Stuve's whisper laughed in the
shadow of the arbor, "if you still are the same

man, you'll do better making a deal with me than
with Ebberly."

"Who says I want to make a deal with anyone?"
asked Johnny.

"You know you have to now . . ." murmured
Stuve.

". . . The Beaches of Lukannon—" rang the
voice of Pat up on the platform, "—the winter
wheat so tall—

> "The dripping, crinkled lichens and the
> sea-fog drenching all!
> "The platforms of our playground, all shin-
> ing smooth and worn!
> "The Beaches of Lukannon—the home where
> we were born!"

"I wasn't sent here by the sea-People," said
Johnny, "to make a deal with you."

"Who's talking about the sea-People?" asked
Stuve. "It's you I want, not them."

"That's even further off the mark," said Johnny.
"I've no reason to make any deal for myself
alone."

"You'd better," said Stuve. "You took yourself
out of leadership of the sea-People to protect your
son, once, didn't you? —Never mind how I know.
You told them you'd never lead them again, but
here you are. And why?"

"Because I'm one of them."

"No, no. . . ." Stuve laughed again, softly,
"you're not one of them—any more than Ebberly,
or I, am like these blunder-headed fools ashore.
You're a leader, Johnny Joya. And you must
lead—it's a compulsion. You may fool yourself

about why you do it, but you do it, anyway. And
what that leading leads to is a final arrangement,
two against one. There are three of us in the world,
Johnny—you, me, and Ebberly. And only room for
two on one side. Right now you've got the choice
of me or Ebberly; but you may not have it a little
later . . ."

He moved backward into the shadows until he
was almost lost in their darkness.

"I'll be waiting," he murmured, so low-voiced
under Pat's singing that for all Johnny's sea-
trained ears the words were hardly distinguish-
able. "Think about it, Johnny. The world's going
smash—on land and sea, alike. Not even Ebberly
knows that. Only you and I know it. And none of
us can stop it. But you and I, Johnny, controlling
Land and Sea in partnership could put if off a little
while—for the length of our own lives, maybe.
That's all I want—peace in my time. We can have
that if we work together, you and I, because only
you and I know about the pattern there is to
things. A pattern like woven thread in a piece of
cloth; and how you pull those threads is how the
pattern goes. Only no one can stop the weaving.
Think about that, Johnny. No one can stop it. But
together, you and I could hold up the finishing of
the pattern for a little while. So think about it . . .
but not too long. I don't want to have to nudge
you . . ."

There was a rustle among the leaves and the
darkness at the far end of the shadowed arbor was
empty. Johnny sat staring at it.

—While, up on the platform, Pat was drawing
the wild, sad anthem of the sea to it's ringing
finish . . .

". . . I met my mates in the morning, a broken, scattered band.
"Men shoot us in the water and club us on the land;
"Men drive us to the Salt House like silly sheep and tame,
"And still we sing Lukannon—before the sealers came.

"Wheel down, wheel down to southward! Oh, Goover-ooska go!
"And tell the Deep-Sea Viceroys the story of our woe;
"Ere, empty as the shark's egg the tempest flings ashore,
"The Beaches of Lukannon shall know their sons no more!"

# 8

A little later, Pat came to collect Johnny from the arbor where he was sitting; they went by walkway to the Estate's private rocket pad some five miles away, and the Entertainment rocket waiting there lifted them for Australia. Lifting high above the curve of the earth they caught up with the dawn and flew into morning. It was three o'clock of a bright Down-Under afternoon when they landed at Entertainment Estates South, north of Sydney, below the bulge of Australia's eastern coast.

Pat, who had been sitting up near the nose of the rocket with Mila Jhan, collected Johnny from a seat near the rear and led him out of the rocket, off the pad, and onto a walkway. A ducted-fan flyer was picking up Mila Jhan. The walkway ran between lines of eucalyptus trees in which koala bears browsed on the leathery limp-hanging leaves, their teddy-bear snouts poking incuriously among the branches, in the process of making their livings, animal-fashion. Otherwise this place was very like the Transportation Estates North, except that the air smelled woody and dry—and also of the salt sea, which bordered one side of the Estates here.

Pat jogged Johnny's elbow and pointed ahead up the walkway. "Look there, now."

Johnny looked and saw one of the round platforms that were terminal points for joining of the walkways.

"When we get there we'll stop for a second," said Pat. "I've got something to show you."

They reached the platform and stepped off onto its unmoving surface a few seconds later. Pat turned to face one of the three walkways branching onward from it and running toward a lofty screen of the enormous king eucalyptus trees, big as the giant California sequoias. The giants at which Johnny looked now towered over three hundred feet in the air.

"Watch," said Pat. "Over the trees—now!"

For a moment as Johnny looked there was only the blue Down-Under sky and the sun approaching mid-afternoon. Then, sweeping suddenly into view above the great treetops, looming over them, blotting out sky and sun at once, flashed the crimson, half-mile-wide shape of a Space Swimmer. At once it was above them. The day was darkened. The koalas paused. The pleasant trees and grass and grounds were all abruptly alike, dyed dark, blood-red, about them—

—And then, it was gone.

It had disappeared, as if the enormous, fantastic, red-rippling shape had never been.

Johnny lowered his eyes slowly from the once more sunlit and empty sky. He looked at Pat.

Pat smiled.

"This way," he said, stepping down onto the walkway that ran toward the trees. Johnny followed.

"It wasn't real then?" Johnny said curiously to Pat, as he caught up and stood beside his cousin. Pat nodded.

"It was real," he answered. "It's just that it wasn't here." He looked steadily at Johnny. "Come and see . . ."

The walkway carried them on between the trees, their trunks like the stringy-barked arms of enormous giants, upthrust through the earth to hold a clenched fist of leaves at the sun. Beyond was a small belt of flowering shrubs, and then they had passed through these to come upon a small, oval salt-water lagoon separated from the blue sea by a small, miniature hill-line of tree and grass.

The dome-shape of what Johnny took to be either an observatory of some sort, or a small, circular auditorium, projected above the water in the center of the lagoon. And the walkway went above the water out to it from the shore.

Pat and Johnny rode out and stepped through the entrance of the domed structure. Within, it was artificially lighted, a depressed circle of seats surrounding a small theater-in-the-round. Behind the top circle of seats was a rim of hallway, and on this, just inside the door, a slim, incredibly beautiful, dark-haired woman was waiting for them. She

was Mila Jhan, Baroness of the Entertainment
Group. Her flyer had evidently gotten her here
before them.

"Johnny," she said, smiling at him when Pat
introduced her. "I know you almost as well as Pat
now—through what he's told me." She did not
offer to shake hands in Lander fashion, and
Johnny wondered whether this was through some
understanding of her own, or whether Pat had
taught her it was a custom almost forgotten by the
sea-People. She was tall, dark—almost fragile
looking in the smallness and perfection of her
boning. Her beauty seemed not so much to be a
matter of face or figure, but of some inner light
shining through the dark lantern of her.

"Did that Space Swimmer belong to you?"
asked Johnny. She shook her head, and her dark
hair moved about the long, olive oval of her face.

"This is all Pat's doing," she said. "I only gave
him what help, influence, facilities, and credit
could give. He'll tell you about it." She put her
hand gently, tenderly, for a moment on Pat's arm.
The gesture was not lost on Johnny.

"This way," said Pat. He turned and led the way
around the rim of hall until he stopped at a section
of back row seats ending on an aisle. At a touch of
his hand four of these swung aside over the
polished flooring of the hall rim to reveal a two-
way escalator ramp leading downwards. They
stepped onto the down side of the ramp and the
seats swung back above them as they descended.
They were carried down until Johnny's sense of
position told him they must be below the lowest
level of the theater area above, and well below the
surface of the lagoon.

They stepped off at last into a ring of working areas encircling a large tank apparently filled with the dark water of the lagoon. There were several people working around various pieces of equipment connected with the tank. One of these, a long-nosed, balding young man, approached them.

"This is Leif Gurdom, Johnny," said Pat. "Leif, this is my cousin, Johnny Joya, whom I told you about." He turned to Johnny. "Leif's in charge here."

"Pleased to meet you," said Leif, offering his hand. He had large, healthy-looking, brown eyes in a long, smiling face. "You're going in the tank, then?"

"Yes, he is," said Pat, before Johnny could speak. "I want him to talk to a Space Swimmer for himself." He turned to the scientist. "You've got one for him haven't you, Leif?"

It was not so much a question as it was a statement. For the first time, Johnny heard in Pat's voice the hard ring of command.

# 9

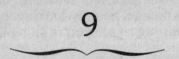

Leif nodded.

"We've locked on to one of the big blues right now," said Leif, "and we've got several more in range of the master unit if that one passes over on us. —This way."

He led them through the mazes of equipment encircling the transparent window of the tank to a waterlock with a double magnetic envelope iris and a pressure chamber between. The envelope faces shimmered like two circles cut from a fresh rainbow. He pointed through the transparent wall beside the waterlock.

"Watch the tank now," he said to Johnny. "*Ready!*" he called over his shoulder, then turned to face the tank himself. Johnny watched with him.

Before Johnny's eyes the shadowed darkness of

the water changed to give way to the star-blazed darkness of space. Johnny felt stirring in him an echo of that original twinge of beckoning excitement that had led him ten years before, with others of the third generation of sea-born, to answer the call of Ebberly's Space Academy ashore.

Now, however, the old excitement touched him lightly. From where he stood outside the tank it was like looking into a globe-shaped cavern of darkness with lights of all colors far off about its walls. A cavern with a distant—very distant—small, circular, brilliant doorway to daylight, which was the sun shrunk to the size of a quarter. Within this cavern, something stirred. It occulted the lights on a portion of the cavern well. Swooping, growing larger, it seemed to approach like a bat-winged shape of blackness and to swell fantastically until it took on color and lay stirring and folding beyond the transparent window. A great, blue field of energized gas, living gas in appearance something between gossamer cloth and that impalpable phosphorescence that glitters, under proper conditions, on the breaking waves of the nighttime sea.

It brought back another memory—a memory of being crammed with five hundred other Cadets in the Space Academy training ship out beyond the orbit of Mars. They had watched the space-sleds with their instructor-operators spreading the net of magnetic fields about another Swimmer as large as this one. That had been more than six years ago.

He had not seen that other Swimmer so close. But he remembered now with sudden inner pain how it had curled up, had shriveled and darkened and died when at last it tried to pass the net and found the charges enclosing it on all sides. He remembered how something inside him had protested and wept, seeing it die this way—how something had reacted inside all of the sea-born aboard the rocket. So that when they got back to the Space Academy on Earth, he had led them easily to the decision to leave the Academy. —A leaving that had ended in war with the Land.

Johnny stiffened a little now—half-expecting in spite of his better knowledge to see the Swimmer before him shrivel and die. But it hung untouched, rippling, but seemingly not progressing, except that the shifting lamps of the stars on the walls of the black cavern around it betrayed its passage.

Johnny felt something small thrust into the palm of his right hand. Brought back with a jerk to the bright laboratory space around him, he lifted the hand and saw in it what looked like a tiny metal moth with two thin, hexagonal wings raised at a forty-five degree angle from the lead-colored, football-shaped body.

"We've got an automated Master Unit out beyond Mars," said Leif beside him. "It sends out, recovers, and services little transceivers like the one you're holding. One just like that is keeping pace with the Swimmer you see imaged there in the tank now. The transceivers use a short-term ion drive which is exhausted at usual Swimmer speeds in half an hour or so. But then another transceiver takes over for it. It receives the Swimmer image and transmits it back to the Master Unit. And it can project images around itself— like the image of the Swimmer you saw projected by a unit flying over the king eucalyptuses, on your way here—and the ones that have appeared over cities ashore here, occasionally. From the Master Unit, transmitted Swimmer images are re-transmitted to a Mars orbital relay, to an Earth orbital relay, and to us here."

Johnny gazed at the Swimmer Unit.

"How much of a time lag in transmission is there?" he asked. "How long ago was that Swimmer doing what I see him doing now?"

"About five seconds ago," said the voice of Leif, behind him. "—You were thinking of the delay in terms of hours, weren't you? But the transmission links are laser beams. The information travels along those tight beams of light at a hundred and eighty-six thousand miles per second. When you go into the tank now, the Swimmer will see your image in space beside him, five seconds after you're in the water."

"Put this on," said Pat, alongside Johnny. Johnny turned to see Pat handing him a small copper skull cap with what looked like a foam-rubber rim. Toward its front edges a ruby-colored crystal glowed.

"This," said Leif, tapping the crystal with a spatulate forefinger, "is something recent in crystallography. It replaces the old model control caps that were developed from the devices used in the original animal telemetry experiments, like W.H. Marshall's Grousar Project in 1960. The crystal replaces the control cap wires that used to have to be surgically inserted into the specific brain areas. It beams the information to, and picks up the electrical impulses from, the motor areas of your brain; and relays them through our transmit-

ter here to the Master Unit controlling the transceiver pacing the Swimmer. And the transceiver
obeys your sub-activity motor impulses to move
you closer to, away from, above, or below the
Swimmer.''

Johnny lifted the cap and put it on his head. The
foam-rubber-like edge seemed to grip him adhe-
sively around the skull and at the temples of his
forehead.

"Here's a waterlung and fins," said Pat. "And a
magnetic envelope."

A few seconds later Johnny penetrated the
inner of the double magnetic irises. He knew that
the sudden pressure of something like twenty feet
underwater—twice atmospheric pressure—was
suddenly closed about him, but inside the magnetic envelope this force was bent around him at
right angles to the surface of his body. He felt
nothing but the cool, wet stroking of the water
against his skin.

For a second or two he swam in water in which
the Swimmer was not visible. Then, abruptly, he
was no longer swimming, but swooping through
the cave of blackness, star-lights, and sun-
entrance he had seen from outside the tank. He
turned his head and saw the half-mile-wide waving blue field of the Swimmer ahead and apparently a little beneath him.

He turned to swim towards the Swimmer as he
would have approached anything in the sea. But
before his swimming body muscles could re-
spond he found himself driving toward the great,
gauzy, shimmering figure. Without warning he
was right above it and it seemed to him the vast,
blue body covered half of all space below him.

A strange feeling was growing in him. At first he thought it was that all this reminded him of swimming in the sea—the freedom of movement in all different ways, up, down, and in any planar direction. And this was true—but what he was feeling was something more. Familiar in a way he could not put his finger on. Familiar but . . . better. He looked around for an explanation in the surroundings, but these told him nothing. He moved on impulse, it seemed, on the drive of thought alone. He skimmed the apparent, endless emptiness of the void and only by the star-lights beyond the undulating back of his great, silent, blue companion could he recognize the fact that they were both in motion.

How fast or how slow was that motion, he wondered? There was no way of telling by the moving star-lights. When he was once more outside the tank Leif might be able to tell him. But he found that he was not interested in asking now, even if he had been equipped with a device to let him do so.

He felt no urge to remember those watching. The strange feeling had grown to a living thing within him. The people outside the tank had dwindled in importance in his mind's eye. They were off there, somewhere, forgotten. —In some awkward, unnatural, alien place of weights and pressures, and constant struggle to exist. While he was here—in the unending reaches of natural freedom.

He had his back to the small and distant sun now and he and the Swimmer fled outward together from it. He moved a little closer above that enormous carpet of undulating blue, strangely

visible in the weak, far-off light of the sun behind them. For a moment, in fact for little more than four seconds, he hung looking at it and then suddenly he saw the speck of a shadow on that part of it directly under him. A tiny shadow with a football-shaped body and barely visible wings.

Instantly, it seemed that he felt something new.

It was gone as soon as he sensed it. But he had no doubt that he had felt it. It was exactly as if he had seen, or heard, or received, some signal to the effect that the Swimmer below him had just wakened to the fact he was above it. He seemed to feel its awareness, through some familiar, but unidentifiable channel of his senses. In the same moment the blue shape began to move away from underneath him. He turned to follow it and the star-lights about them both altered with their movement.

He felt the return of the excitement of his original feeling, and with it a sense of purposefulness that seemed to flow toward him either from the Swimmer or—strangely—from the direction of their flight.

The sense of purposefulness which he felt rose sharply. It sang up abruptly to an intolerable pitch like a mounting siren of warning. He flung up his arms instinctively as if to protect himself against some invisible barrier before them—

And the Swimmer disappeared.

Johnny was left alone in the star cavern. But not completely alone. A memory clung to him like the afterimage superimposed on the retina after a sudden strong flaring of light has disappeared. There had been a split second in which it seemed he had looked through to a place beyond this

present spot. A place where the stars were
positioned differently. Where a larger, whiter sun
for a fraction of a second washed across the blue
surface of the Swimmer, now plunging away from
him at a speed no ion-drive instrument could
match.

A pressure of other forces had filled his familiar
but indefinable sense which had been active since
he had joined the image of the Swimmer. A pattern of difference—and suddenly understanding
washed through him like a wave of coolness.

The feeling, the familiar, new, tantalizing but
yet unidentified feeling he had begun to sense
from his first moment in the tank—all at once it
was clear to him what he had been touching. —It
was the same thing he had felt in that moment in
the berg-Home when he had touched the dreaming Tomi and something like a spark had jumped
between them. Only this time it was the actual
thing he had experienced, instead of a second-
hand awareness of it.

It was the maze outside the analog—the place of
golden girders—the other universe, outside the
space-time one that was comprehensible to ordinary human senses, the greater universe through
which the Space Swimmers passed, leaping
light-years of distance in no time at all. Once
Johnny had felt it, through Tomi. Now, again, he
had felt it in this tank.

Just for a moment he had sensed it—and then it
went as the Swimmer vanished.

He found himself floating in dark water, looking through a transparent wall in a brightly lit
circle of structure where people stood watching
him like some strange creature captured from a

different world. Feeling drained, unusually clumsy and heavy, Johnny turned and swam with effortful physical movements back to the iris of the waterlock. He climbed through and a moment later stood, stripped of his magnetic envelope on the wet floor of the laboratory.

"Well?" demanded Pat.

Johnny turned slowly to face him.

"This was why," Johnny said, "you went along with the plan of Maytig and the Sea Captains to bring me back to lead the People."

"Not just the People," said Pat. His face was tight. "Did you feel anything when you were in the tank there, chasing the Swimmer? I mean did you touch—*touch*—something like you'd never touched before?"

Their eyes met and held.

"Yes," said Johnny.

"Then you know," said Pat. He did not look away from his cousin. "I've never changed my mind from the very beginning, Johnny. I still think that the Land is part of us—and we can't afford to cut ourselves off from any part of our human race that's there. It's not their fault they're the way they are, ashore. It's just that they've given up because it seemed there was no place to go—no hope of the stars they once dreamed of reaching. And so, for six years here ashore I've been trying to find that hope again for them. But we're up against a blank wall now."

"Blank wall?" said Johnny.

"Tell him, Leif," Pat ordered.

The scientist leaned forward eagerly as Johnny turned to him.

"Do you know what they are?" Leif asked. "The

Space Swimmers, I mean?" Johnny shook his
head. "Well, just as we human beings are essentially water in an envelope of solid chemicals, the
Swimmers are gas in an envelope of magnetic
forces—forces like the forces of the pressure envelopes you sea-People wear underwater. Only
their magnetic forces let them hook in somehow
to a whole network of magnetic forces existing
outside our ordinary space-time universe, magnetic forces which we think have to do with the
powerful, if diffuse, magnetic field of our own
galaxy—a field with a flow of some three quintil-
lions of amperes—"

He broke off.

"You do follow me?" he asked, anxiously.
Johnny nodded.

"We theorize, then," said Leif, urgently, "that
there's something like a complex network of
linear subforces linked to this magnetic field—
and that somehow the Swimmers can tap these
forces, which exist outside the physical universe
as we know it, and pass from point to point in the
physical universe instantanously. No matter how
far apart those points are."

Johnny nodded again.

"—But the thing is—" Leif winced, almost as if
at a physical pain, "here in this lab we can
examine the Swimmers only as far as they pertain
to the physical space-time universe. We can't
examine them when they leave that universe for
the complex of subforces, because our instruments themselves belong completely to the
space-time universe. So, we're licked. —Except
for people like you . . . and Pat."

"Pat and I?" Johnny looked narrowly at the long-faced man.

"—and the rest of your sea-People," said Leif. "I've been in that tank many times, with Swimmers in contact. So have most of us who've been working here. We don't feel a thing—we don't, as Pat says, *touch* anything—when the Swimmers 'pass over'; disappear, I mean. But Pat's always felt it, and now you. So there's no other conclusion possible. It seems you sea-born people have a sensitivity to the magnetic subforces that we land-born don't."

There was a second's long silence in the lab.

"You see?" said Pat, finally, staring steadily at Johnny. "The Land can't find what it needs. The Sea is going to have to find it for them, if either Land or Sea are going to survive. You heard Ebberly about the *salmonella* mutation. Sooner or later some psychotic, irresponsible element will get their hands on it and poison the sea. And I don't doubt that the People now have a weapon equally deadly, to use against the land. Maytig as much as admitted so when I met her with the Sea Captains. There's only one way out."

He stopped, looking tightly at Johnny. But Johnny looked back without answering.

"Land and Sea have got to work together—or destroy each other," said Pat. "We've got to start it—we sea-People. We've got to do what the Landers can't. Find them the star route. Trade them the other worlds they need, for the sea we've got to have. It's the only way, the *only* way, Johnny. Because it's not true that we're different sorts of human beings, on sea and shore. Maybe there have been sea-changes in the generations afloat—but that doesn't make them all right, and the Land all wrong. If the Land's so rotten, what was it ashore gave birth to three thousand years of music—to three thousand years of paintings, books, and buildings—three thousand years of great thought and great action? I tell you they're the same, Johnny, on land and sea—the same people! Maybe with different shells of flesh and blood, but with the same human spirit in them, fighting, crying to break free! Johnny—do you hear me? Do you understand what I'm saying?"

"You're saying," said Johnny, without emotion, "that the Hunting of the People has to go on. That the *salmonella* mutation has to hang like a sword over our heads. —All while we try to do in months or weeks what nobody's ever dreamed of doing before for people who've offered us only death and exile ashore."

"I know!" said Pat. His eyes blazed and his voice broke out so fiercely that Mila Jhan stepped to him, putting a hand once more on his arm as if to hold him back. He did not move, but neither did he seem to feel her touching him. "But there's no other way! If you can think of any other way, then you find it, Johnny! *You find it!*"

On Johnny Joya, hereditary leader of the Sea, rested the fate of the world.

# 10

The Sea Captain for the Great Barrier Reef area had arranged for a smallboat to be left at Entertainment Estates South. Johnny took it the next day; and headed back along the line of route that his sea-born instincts, like those of seal, dolphin, and whale, told him would bring him eventually to the current position of Maytig's sea-lab.

Rushing through the blue twilight of the depths he tried once more, and without much hope to summon up the clear images from the analog. But only a chaotic kaleidoscope of probablities responded. He had abandoned the analog for its real world counterpart now; and there was no going back.

Moreover, the analog had essentially fulfilled its purpose. It had shown him the way to his four fuses to Armageddon; which were Maytig's Ring

of Fire, Ebberly's offer of a shore sanctuary for the
People, Stuve's dark offer of a partnership in a
world kingdom of Land and Sea combined—and
that final cryptic fuse *"in sea, on land"* that had
turned out to be the sea-born Pat's land-based
research into the secrets of the Space Swimmers.

The worst of the four, the most dangerous, was
Stuve. For Stuve, apparently, was a genius of ex-
traordinary order; enough so, even though land-
born, to see as well as Johnny the red glow of
Armageddon on the horizon of the future. With
Stuve in the picture, Johnny could not, as he
would have liked, taken an independent route to
head off all four fuses. To overmatch Stuve, he
must choose one of the fuses already in existence
and hope to twist it so as to stave off the threaten-
ing explosion of the end.

The choices were not pretty ones.

To take the way of Maytig and the People was
an instinctive answer. But the Ring of Fire could
lead only to drowned millions of square miles of
land; and dead sea-bottom upthrust, reeking in
the sun with the death of all that had belonged to
its former watery environment.

To choose Ebberly's terms would only thrust off
Armageddon a little further into the future; and
only at the price of blunting and killing the development of the sea-senses in the sea-children.

To make a deal with Stuve meant the life and
development of the fourth-generation children,
free in the sea. But then, Armageddon more surely
for being delayed, in such measure as even the
fourth generation could not handle.

Lastly, Pat's way meant to gamble the lives of
the sea-People under the threat not only of Eb-

berly and Stuve, but of Hunters and bacterial death—against the faint hope of doing within a few months what had never been hoped for in less than years of research—the extracting of the secret of faster-than-light travel from the Space Swimmers.

But one of these four choices Johnny must make. And he must choose right, for there would be no second chance. Rushing through the twilight of the hundred-fathom depth, Johnny sought with all his sea-instincts, with all the experience that building the analog had given him, for a clue to the proper answer—and was reminded of his fourth-generation hole card, which was Tomi.

Through Tomi's fourth-generation abilities, perhaps the choices could be tested, in some way, and a clue to the right one found. Thinking about the boy, now, he drove north and east until the lights of the sea-lab finally loomed ahead of him.

Baldur and Conquistador came to meet him as he slowed to enter the magnetic envelope of the docking iris. He greeted them and went on in. Maytig and Tomi, he was told in the lab, were in Maytig's office. He went there, and was arrested, as he reached for the office door, by the sound of combined boy-and-woman laughter from inside.

Suddenly, unexpectedly, there swept through him the irrational but mighty emotion of he who hears, secretly, the sound of happiness between those he loves. Suddenly, he was weakened by the powerful sweep of his own, personal emotions that threatened to carry him away from the larger problems of his duty into an area where he would

be concerned for only those close to him—and
damn the rest of the world.

He shook the feeling off with an effort; and
stepped through into the office. Tomi and Maytig
looked up from Maytig's desk.

"Dad!" cried Tomi. "You're back! Conquistador and Baldur have been here almost a week.
They came in, just like I said."

"I saw them outside when I docked," said
Johnny. He came up to the desk. "What's this?"

They had been sketching, evidently, what
looked like the picture of a squid. At the bottom of
the sketch, upside down from Johnny's point of
view, was printed the word, *Mugger*.

"Know who that is?" Tomi asked. He grinned.

Johnny gazed at it. The sketch had been made
by some skilled hand . . . probably Maytig's. The
tentacles were in proportion and the single eye
showing was properly placed. However, some ir-
reverent stylus point had added long, sweeping
lashes over the cephalopod eye, so that the whole
creature seemed to simper up from the page at
them.

"He's the deep-sea ceph the lab's been following and studying!" said Tomi. "I named him
Mugger, after the Mugger of Mugger-Ghat—you
know, the crocodile in *The Undertakers*, the Kip-
pling story? —I mean, he doesn't look like a
crocodile, of course, but he grumbles around
down there on the deep bottom, never having
enough to eat, like the Mugger in the story."

"And," said Maytig, looking at Johnny with a
curiously penetrating gaze, "your son talks to
him."

Something in Johnny woke to sudden alertness.

But he hid his reactions. There was no harm, he thought, in finding out what Maytig knew, before he gave his own knowledge away.

"So did I when I was his age," he said.

"No," said Maytig, and there was no mistaking the diamond brilliance of her gaze, now. "I mean Tomi *talks* to this deep sea cephalopod—the way you'd talk to a dolphin—or Conquistador." She waited a moment, as if waiting for Johnny's reaction. "Do you want to see for yourself?"

"Very much so," said Johnny.

"I'll go get Conquistador—he helps translate!" said Tomi, and dashed out. Twenty minutes later Johnny, Tomi, Maytig, and Conquistador—all of them including the killer whale (for this was beyond his normal diving depth) wearing respirators, magnetic envelopes, and resolving goggles to match the infra-red lamps they carried—were descending toward the sea-bottom three miles below.

In darkness they descended past the two-mile limit, and after a while Tomi announced he could feel the bottom near him. A few seconds later the two third-generation adults felt their own sea-senses "feeling" the red clay and ooze below them. Maytig altered the angle of the lamp she carried so that the light, visible to the humans wearing the resolving glasses, but invisible to the deep-sea creatures, was cast more directly downward.

A few moments later the light revealed something below them. And this shortly exposed itself as a wide and level plain with what seemed to be a flat surface of fine gray silt. A few grotesque-headed fish with fine barbels and phosphorescent

"lights" glowing at the barbel tips, or in a line along their bodies, seemed to hang suspended in nothingness at various distances.

It was an eerie, soundless, motionless country, its unlimited, unchanging range in eternal darkness, except for the small candles of such lights as they had brought down with them; and which they now left hanging in midwater above as they descended the rest of the way to the bottom under the infra-red beams.

"There he is now!" Tomi called through his mask diaphragm to Johnny and Maytig. "I knew he'd be right about here. —Watch yourself, now, Mugger!"

Turning a little to his right, Johnny caught sight on the silt plain of an enormous, cable-like mass of ten living, incredible tentacles. They were orange-colored in the resolved light. Hidden behind these stirring, giant appendages at first, but emerging into view as the intruders approached, came the body of the cephalopod, shaped like a fat rocket. —Which in fact it was, since the Mugger, like other Cephalopoda, could propel himself by jetting water backward through a muscular funnel in the mantle of his body. —Tomi's last few words, Johnny now saw, were prompted by one of the enormous tentacles, uncoiling in the direction of the boy and the suddenly dwarfed-looking killer whale.

Tomi had brought along a sonic rifle—a toy in appearance compared to the two-hundred-foot length of living, tentacled flesh before him. But he pointed it now and the tentacle jerked back like the hand of a child caught sneaking something sweet from a candy counter.

"He's really pretty friendly," Tomi's voice came through his mask, distorted and water-born to Johnny's ears. "He just hates to pass up anything he can eat. It's because he's so old."

Johnny, looking at the bottom-dwelling monster, understood. The Mugger had lived too long. He had outgrown his ability to forage for the vast amounts of food his tremendous bulk required. It was this same eventual, desperate hunger that caused his kind at last to rise toward the surface and attack the great whales, or any other edible being they could find.

"He's all right now!" Tomi called. "Come on, Dad, Maytig!"

Johnny and Maytig approached. With the killer whale alongside him, Tomi swam unconcernedly over the middle of the nest of Brobdingnagian tentacles. And, not without a cool feeling at the back of his neck, Johnny followed with Maytig beside him. By the time they caught up with his son and Conquistador, they were poised in mid-water, some ten feet above an orange bulk the size of an old-fashioned midget submarine, and an eye the size of an automobile hub cap was staring up at them.

"Look, Mugger," said Tomi, "this is my father."

The killer whale beside them moved slightly in the water. The fantastic eye below continued to stare upward.

"He doesn't understand what a 'father' is," said Tomi, "I should have thought of that. He gets the idea you belong with me, though and he's not supposed to eat you. He's pretty intelligent, actually. Maybe I ought to call it wise, not intelligent, because it really comes just from being so old. He likes meeting anyone interesting. The only trouble is he can't keep his mind on anything but how hungry he is for very long. He'll do some tricks for me, though, if I promise to send some food down to him."

"Tricks?" asked Johnny.

"Would you like to see him stand on tiptoe?"

"Yes," said Johnny. "Yes, I would indeed."

"Up, Mugger!" The great living structure underneath them stirred; and man, woman, boy, and killer whale, backed off. "All the way up!" ordered Tomi. "I'll get you a white shark, forty feet long, bigger than Conquistador, and sink him down to you here. I know where I can kill one like that. Up, Mugger! Now—right now! Up!"

Slowly, the giant cephalopod was rising. For a second it seemed as if the effort was too great for it to attempt. Then a heavy current in the water rocked all four watchers and the Mugger shot upwards as lightly as a feather—up and up, until his body threatened to vanish into the darkness above the infra-red lamps they had left burning above to illuminate the scene. And his longest tentacle's tip trailed just above the silt, which was once more settling after being stirred up in a cloud by the jet from the Mugger's funnel. Two hundred feet up . . . up . . . until he towered like a fifteen-story office building over their heads.

Then, slowly, he settled once more to the ocean floor.

"Good Mugger!" said Tomi. He turned to his father and Maytig. "We'd better go now."

They went. The ascent was a quiet one. Johnny was thinking deeply. They returned to the sea-lab and released a grateful killer whale from his waterlung and magnetic envelope. He shot off toward the surface and vanished.

"I'll go after him," said Tomi, through his mask. "I'll take him hunting or something to make it up to him."

The boy also disappeared. Johnny and Maytig re-entered the lab and got rid of their own pressure envelopes and waterlungs. They went back to Maytig's office.

"You weren't surprised," Maytig challenged Johnny, staring across the desk at him, once they were seated. "You knew Tomi talked to sea-creatures besides the dolphin People and his killer whale."

Johnny nodded.

"He used to talk to the wild killers and the antarctic seals, when we were at the berg-Home," he answered.

"How does he do it?"

Johnny stared at her. The question had jolted him severely. He had made an assumption—and apparently it was unfounded.

"Don't you know?" he asked. "You're the expert on the People."

"No." She shook her head. "All I know is that it isn't telepathy. Did you know that much, yourself?"

"Yes," said Johnny. "There's more to it than telepathy. He talks to the beasts out loud; and he says he 'hears' them answering him, in words. It's always been that way with him, and he doesn't see anything strange about it. But there's just one trouble." Johnny looked bleakly at her. "The beasts tell him more than they could possibly know in their own right."

"More than they know?" Maytig frowned.

"I don't mean the dolphins or the killers," said Johnny. "They've got brains comparable to our own. But when a leopard or a Weddel seal expresses himself with the intelligence and vocabulary of a ten-year-old boy—whose intelligence isn't exactly bad for his age—"

"You don't have to tell me that," said Maytig drily. "Go on."

"—Then there's something more than telepathy involved. It's as if a migrating bird were able to answer you in biological detail about the physical mechanisms involved in its urge to migrate."

He stopped. She sat looking at him.

"Well, go on," she said. "What is it, then, Tomi's got? Whatever it is, it must be latent in the rest of his generation!" Her voice rose, fiercely. "We need to know. We've got to find out—"

"Then," Johnny broke in, heavily, "you really don't understand it at all, either?"

The fierceness went out of her. She looked at him in dismay.

"You mean you don't have some idea, yourself?" she demanded.

"All I know," said Johnny, "is that it seems to have something to do with an ability to identify—and I don't just mean empathize—but identify, completely, right down to the biological roots, with another living creature. With that kind of identification, evidently, anything as surface as language or attitude becomes unimportant in communication."

He paused, looking at her unsmilingly.

"I'd have mentioned this ability of Tomi's to you myself," he said. "But when I came back and saw you and him playing with it, I thought you'd identified it, and already understood it yourself. I was going to ask you a question about it—particularly since it's important right now."

"Important?" she asked. "Why?"

She had tensed; and he read her sudden worry in the way she sat looking at him. He checked his own impulse to dive directly into the question that had occurred to him when he had seen Tomi commanding the Mugger.

"Let me tell you what Ebberly offered us, first," he said.

He told her. He also handed her the vial of the *salmonella* mutation. That did not disturb her. But when he came to the matter of the People moving ashore, she interrupted with a gasp of sheer fury.

"Go ashore!" she cried. "But the fourth-generation children won't ever develop if they have to leave the sea! We'd die as a People—we'd revert to being Landers. Johnny, we can't do that!"

He nodded.

"Well," he said in a neutral voice, "we've got another offer. On my way home I came through Entertainment Estates South, you know; and it turned out Pat had something to show me there . . ."

He told her about the Space Swimmer research and his own experience with the blue Swimmer in the tank.

She listened attentively. It was as if she drank in information not merely through her ears but through the whole structure of her body. A sort of *Gestalt* listening. But when he was done she sat still for a moment; and then slowly shook her head.

"No . . ." she said; and sighed deeply, "even if we brought the lab to the sea where we could work on it. Even if we could take the experimentation further than this man Leif and his crew have been able to—there's no real reason to hope we could get the answer where they've failed. The answer might be beyond any human powers of investigation. These Swimmers may be completely out of context with solid life forms like ourselves. We can't risk the People and all the fourth-generation children on a wild chance of success."

"But maybe it wouldn't be so wild a chance," said Johnny. She looked at him, puzzled.

"We might have an interpreter in our midst," said Johnny. "I mean, Tomi. Doesn't it seem to you possible that the boy who can talk to a darkness-living, deep-sea monster like that cephalopod, might be able to talk as well to one of the Space Swimmers?"

She stared at him. —And she went on staring. She did not answer, although he waited.

"That's not just a rhetorical question," he said, at last, sharply. "You're the expert on the People, and the fourth-generation children. All I know is my son. You've seen how Tomi can talk with just about anything in the sea. Can he communicate with the Space Swimmers if he's given a chance to—or can't he?"

She opened her lips as if to answer, then closed them again. Slowly, she shook her head.

"If I had time to study him . . . but I don't," she almost whispered. "How can I tell you,

Johnny? Tomi's completely outside anything I've
known in the fourth generation up until now. I
can't tell whether he'd be able to talk to Space
Swimmers, or not!"

He nodded, not happily.

"I was afraid that'd be your answer," he said.
"Ever since you asked me if I knew what it was
Tomi had."

He looked around the office, then shrugged.

"Well," he said, flatly. "It seems as if I'll have to
go ahead without an answer—and gamble. It's the
one choice of action with some hope to it. I'll get
in touch with Pat right away about moving his lab
to the sea. And we'll see. . . . what we'll see."

# 11

Three weeks later, at the sea-lab, the equipment from Leif's lab had been brought out from Entertainment Estates South and hooked up; and the combined labs were in working order underwater. The tank in which Johnny had had his experience with the blue Swimmer now plugged the double depth of the space in the center of the two Homes, one superimposed upon the other, that had made up the original sea-lab like two circular slices of canned pineapple fastened together. The tank fitted into the circular opening as a checker piece might plug the hole in two such pineapple rings. A special entrance in the bottom face of the tank had been constructed for Conquistador. He was already inside it now, wearing a respirator and swimming around uneasily with one eye on Tomi, whom Johnny located just outside the tank,

putting on his waterlung and magnetic envelope,
and preparing to enter the water with the killer
whale.

"Going to watch?" asked Tomi in the moment
before he slipped the faceplate of his waterlung
up into position over his face.

"That's right," said Johnny.

"Good!" said the boy. He jerked the plate up,
turned, and went through the iris in a running
dive, activating his magnetic envelope as he did
so. Johnny saw him, through the transparent wall
of the tank, shoot out into the midst of the water
and immediately be joined by Conquistador, unhappy in envelope and waterlung. Tomi began
stroking the sides of the big cetacean; and Johnny
knew the boy was talking soothingly to the
killer.

"Tomi in the tank already?" asked Leif, coming
up with Maytig. Maytig had been aloof with him
at first, but the balding, intense-minded Lander
had penetrated this defense within minutes.
Their common ground, which might be called the
research attitude, was too strong. Johnny felt an
odd sensation, seeing them close together now. It
could not, he thought, be anything as farfetched
as jealousy.

"Yes," he answered Leif now. "Tomi just went
in."

"Well," said Leif, "I think we're ready." He
turned and waved to some of his own technicians
standing further back at the control equipment
connected with the tank. Then he turned once
more to the curving glass wall beyond which they
could now all see Conquistador patrolling the

inner circumference with Tomi holding still in the lighted center of the water. "—Tomi!"

Leif had activated the cordless phone clipped to the lapel of his white jacket. Tomi's voice answered at once from a floor speaker in the base of the transparent tank wall.

"I'm here, Leif."

"Can you hear me all right?"

"Sure," said Tomi's voice. "Conquistador's not too happy in here, though. —Where's the Space Swimmer?"

The sudden ringing of an alarm bell shattered the concentration of his thoughts. Abruptly the bell ceased and a voice called from a speaker back behind the equipment.

"Contact!" said the voice. "*Contact!* Patrolboat One to Lab. Hunter passing at a hundred and fifty miles northeast of lab—in air, altitude two thousand feet, speed four-fifty, inclination of path to patrol circle twenty-two degrees."

"I'll go check on the plot cube, just in case that Hunter turns in close," said Maytig. She turned and went off toward the Communications Room, center for the patrol of smallboats that were in constant motion in the waters about the lab at fifteen-and twenty-mile distances.

"—Tomi," Leif was saying, "we're about to lock you in with one of the Swimmers, now. You'd better hang on to Conquistador in case it scares him."

"I've got him," came back Tomi's voice from the base speaker. In the tank, Johnny could see that his son was now clinging to the holding strap of the killer's harness.

"Now!" said Leif.

The illumination in the tank blacked out into darkness and the glowing lights of stars and the far-distant doorway of the sun. There was the movement of an occulting shape and a second after that a powerful, invisible blow against the transparent side of the tank that made the whole sea-lab sing and vibrate.

"No!" shouted the voice of Tomi from the speaker. "It's all right, Conquistador! I tell you it's all right! Do you hear me?"

"Trouble, Tomi?" demanded Leif.

"He's all right now—I think," answered Tomi. "It was the lights going out. He's afraid of things he can't see. It comes from dreams when he was small." Tomi, Johnny thought, was of course not speaking of actual dreams, since the dolphin tribe to which the killer whales belong never slept, in the human sense of the word. Their respiratory centers were under conscious, voluntary control, so that unconsciousness meant drowning or asphyxiation. Tomi must mean some other sort of dreaming. Johnny made a mental note to ask Tomi about this—

"All right," Leif said beside him. "Look now, Tomi, down toward the part of the tank where I'm standing. There's your Space Swimmer."

Outside the tank, Johnny looked also. Distant and small beyond the transparent wall was the tiny form of a Space Swimmer, blue in color. It swelled rapidly in size as they watched as the transceiver linked with Tomi began to converge on the gas creature.

Suddenly it seemed to explode in size until it filled the lower part of the tank. The eyes of those watching, by now adjusted to the distant light of the sun, saw Conquistador shy away from it and go blundering once more against the far side of the tank.

"—I've got to let him out!" Tomi called, panting. "He's too scared!"

"All right!" called Leif, but with a note of disappointment in his voice, to Johnny's ears. "If he rams around in there, he's going to wreck the whole laboratory. Let him out and then come back here in the lab, yourself."

Tomi's voice rang from the base speaker.

"But you aren't going to quit!" it cried. "Wait'll I let Conquistador out. I want to talk to that Swimmer!"

"You can't talk without Conquistador to help you, can you?"

"I think I can. . . ." Tomi's voice trailed off. A section in the bottom of the star-bright universe blanked out to gray momentarily and the flukes of the killer whale vanished through it. A moment later the gray blank disappeared and Tomi swam back into position above the blue rippling expanse of the Swimmer.

"Now—" he began.

The fresh clamor of the alarm bell drowned out his voice.

"Contact!" cried a voice from the alarm speaker. "Contact, Patrol Four. Hunter at a hundred and ten miles, forty-fathom depth—"

Another voice crowded in while the first was still speaking.

"Contact!" it shouted. "Contact! Patrol Two. Hunter, ninety miles, surface—"

The voices of the other patrol smallboat pilots

chimed in. Suddenly they ceased and Maytig's voice came over the speaker.

"Johnny? Johnny, there're thirty or forty Hunter ships coming in at once from all points surrounding. Johnny—"

"All right," he called back. His mind was working smoothly and cleanly as it always did under stress. He picked up the threads of a plan he had half-considered earlier. "Put our extra smallboats out with the ones already there, but haul them in close to the lab. —As if we were tightening up for a last-ditch defense. But I want all the available men with me now down at the cargo hatch. We're going to fill those cargo pods with sea-water, and take them down to bottom—"

He glanced at the current image of the sea-bottom beneath the lab—a mile-and-a-half deep below them were the tops of an undersea mountain range with the deep and narrow canyons of a drowned land where there was no weather to erode and simplify the wrinkling of the crustal folds.

"We'll see if we can't draw the Hunter ships after us," he said, "or at least divide them. They don't like anything less than heavy odds on their side. If we can split them in half, even, the half left above will probably hesitate about attacking.

"Why should they follow the pods?" asked the voice of Maytig, worried.

"Inflated with sea-water and clustered around one of the smallboats to hide it, they'll look to the Hunter instruments like some new sort of underwater ship. A big one. Together the pods ought to look as large as a submarine warship. And the fact we're leaving the lab behind and running away with something like that will make the pod-shape look both valuable and vulnerable. Some, anyway, will follow us. In fact, I think most will."

He did not wait for further discussion, but turned and left at a run for the cargo section in the bottom level of the lab.

Five minutes later, he had been joined by all the available third-generation sea-born fighting men in the lab, and they were dropping downward now through the pitch darkness, their sea-sense alert to feel the approach of the bottom.

"How soon before the first ones should catch us?" he asked over his phone to sea-lab.

"Maybe ten, twelve minutes," answered Maytig.

They could *feel* the bottom approaching now. They were making their descent utterly without lights, relying on their sea-senses. From these came a mental image. It was sight-without-sight. But the human mind trained to think in terms of lighted or unlighted objects, built up an imaginative picture very like a photographic negative of their new surroundings. It grew in their minds now, like a montage in black and silver; and there was a silent, eerie beauty to it. Artists of the sea-born had painted their individual interpretations of it—for no two of the People saw it exactly alike. Pat had written—and this was the most successful of attempts to capture its values—music about it. —But there was no time to enjoy the conceptual beauty of the undersea mountain range to which they were falling now.

"Steer for that canyon," clicked Johnny to the

pilot of the smallboat inside the pods. They altered course slightly. Now, the looming, uprising silver-black peaks of undersea mountains taller than Everest were lifting toward them. They came swiftly, seeming to approach the descending mass instead of the other way around. What Johnny had indicated was a canyon splitting a narrow tableland of grey silt, a plateau-like section of mountain top a little lower than the surrounding peaks, which seemed to poke up and surround them as they came down toward the narrow cleft in the silted, level plain.

"Check!" ordered Johnny. And the pilot of the smallboat touched his controls to bring the pod to a halt above the canyon, which was too narrow to allow the bulk of the pod to go down into it.

"All right," clicked Johnny to the others. Already they could feel the distant water-shock of the approaching Hunters. "Deflate the pods, and take them down at least another twenty fathoms. Then find an open spot where you can inflate again. —And come back up."

"After that, what?" asked the identifiable clicking of Yves Amant, one of the ex-Cadets among the fighting men.

"Then," said Johnny, "we hold up in the crevices of the rock around this strip of plain, and wait for the Hunters. When I tell you, come out fighting." They moved to obey.

It was well they moved swiftly. They had barely fitted themselves into their niches, when the first Hunter ship appeared. They saw the firefly gleam of its powerful visible-light beam, like the light of an aircraft on land, high overhead.

It circled cautiously, descending. Shortly it was

joined by another light, and then another. Like carrion crows descending on a corpse, the ships of the Hunters dropped down around the narrow, long-reaching mouth of the canyon that was too small for them to enter. Below them in the canyon, the pod would be sending back echoes of its inflated bulk to their instruments, puzzling them as to how something many times larger than themselves could have gone where they could not follow, and further exciting their bloodthirstiness.

The radio receivers of the sea-born fighters' masks were filled with the scrambled code of the Hunters talking it over among themselves. Gradually the talk ceased. A minute or so of silence went by, and then the hatch of one of the ships opened, to let out a figure in mask, envelope, and heavily armed with rifle, sonic pistol, and shark knife. Another such figure followed him—and then they were coming out of all the ships.

As Johnny had planned, they were taking the only possible way to follow the pod-shape—having probably dared each other over their radios to the point where they would attempt it. They were going down personally into the crack.

Johnny waited. He counted. All the ships but one now had disgorged at least one swimmer—there was forty-seven of them in all. The last ship apparently was not going to give up its occupants.

The white-light lamps of the Hunters, this close to the silt plain, badly illuminated the scene from below. Clouds of silt had been stirred up to make an underwater fog.

"All right," clicked Johnny to the sea-born. "Shark knives only to start with. Let's go."

Like silent shadows the seventeen sea-born fighting men launched themselves from their rock cracks, out across the level plain of silt toward their forty-seven heavily armed enemies.

# 12

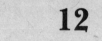

Their powerful, ocean-trained muscles driving them at the sprint speed of Olympic swimmers of a hundred years before, six inches above the loose gray silt of the plain, the sea-born shot silently out of the darkness into the lighted midst of the Hunters clustered about the lips of the canyon. And closed with their attackers.

Since the world's waters had first flooded this arena of darkness and silence, a mile-and-a-half below the sunlight and air of the world above, the Hunters' ships sat and slumbered undisturbed. Now, without warning, it was transformed into a cockpit of hand-to-hand combat. Struggling figures threshed silt into suspension in the floodlight-lit water; where it hung, heavy as smoke, through which the black shapes of swimmers floundered and tangled and locked, driving shark knives home, as often below the original surface level of the silt as above it.

It was one glaring, dark-fogged nightmare, split momentarily by the glare of the lights from the surrounding Hunter ships. The sea-born fought in silence, but the Landers shouted at each other, raved, and cried out over their radio circuits. If the forty-seven of them had fought together as a unit—if they had been fighters to begin with in-stead of what they were, soft and untrained men for the most part, whose hobby happened to be Hunting rather than erotic art—if there had been one leader among them—they would undoubt-edly have smothered the seventeen fighting men from the sea by the sheer superior weight of their numbers. But they lost the chance to fight sensi-bly in the first few moments of the battle, so that from then on it became man-on-man.

Man-on-man, the sea-born would have been superior in weight and strength and reflexes, even ashore. Here in the ocean, their advantage was multiplied. Here and there, by the sheer chance of battle, four or five Landers were able to throw themselves on one of the fighting men of the sea at once, to grind him down into a flurry of water-born silt, and dispatch him with multiple, clumsy thrusts of their shark knives, in that melee where it was neither safe nor practical to use guns. Here and there, occasionally, one of the Landers proved to be an expert swimmer, a knowledgeable knife user, trained in body and mind. But there were only a handful of these and they could not find each other in the murk to fight intelligently together.

Johnny met and killed one Hunter immediately.

Then he was surrounded by half a dozen, who forced him down into the silt, where he twisted and struck upward at them. Abruptly he was up out of the silt, with four of them enclosing him. He drove his knife into one figure and tore a face mask of another free of the waterlung to which it was attached. Others poured in on him, but his mind was clear now of everything but the task of killing and the cool, white lightning of his thoughts went always a few seconds before him, calculating the moves of his enemies, even as they moved to make them. He twisted clear, and avoided, and struck; and twisted and struck again.

Around him, and around all the arena of the battleground, drifted close the grotesque, strange fish of the lower deep, drawn by the water-born vibrations of the struggle. Great-jawed, hump-backed, and file-thin bodies, with barbels trailing strange phosphorescent lights, or lighted in rows along their pale sides, they gathered about the area. Miles away in darkness—an incredible distance to sense the disturbance by land standards, the Mugger also felt the vibrations. —And thought of food. A humpback or a cow blue whale, perhaps, in a death struggle with a lesser member of one of the Mugger's own race—both of whom would be eatable. —And came gliding swiftly toward the scene like some great, silent, two-hundred-foot wraith.

But now, the battle was almost over. Some Landers were already trying to re-enter their ships and escape in emulation of the one ship which had let out no swimmers, and had already fled. The sea-born intercepted these Hunters, caught

and killed them. The fight became a butchery. But
still the sea-born killed—for the men they exe-
cuted were ghouls, driven only by a perverted
appetite for murder. And each one knifed now
meant one less to track down helpless sea-People
in other oceans.

. . . After a while, the battlefield was still. The
silt began to settle again. The surviving fighting
men of the sea began to see each other, as if
through a gradually thinning mist, among the
floating bodies, bloodied inside their mag envelopes by the vital fluid which the envelopes
would not allow to escape. Johnny counted his
men. There were twelve of them. They had lost
four of the third generation.

They gathered the bodies of their own dead,
leaving the Lander corpses for the Mugger and his
comrades of the dark. They took the bodies aboard
one of the Hunter ships, recalled the smallboat
from among the pods in the canyon on its automatic pilot, and returned to the sea-lab above. All
but two had been wounded—but except for the
four who were dead—none were wounded seri-
ously. Johnny was one of the two unmarked. He
left the rest in the cargo section of the sea-lab to
have their wounds tended and went directly back
to the control area outside the tank, pulling off his
faceplate as he went.

He strode up to where he had been standing
when Maytig had called him. Tomi was still in the
tank. Leif was standing where he had been before,
and Maytig was beside him. They turned and Leif
started a little at this sudden apparition of a tall,
wet-faced figure, still clothed in black coldwater

suit, weapons, and water gear, the faceplate of his waterlung hanging down on his chest.

"You're back," said Leif. "Was it bad—"

"We came out all right," said Johnny briefly. He read the question in Maytig's eyes and added shortly, "We lost four." He turned back to the tank, gesturing at the figure of Tomi, which still hung above the rippling blue expanse of the Space Swimmer. "What's been happening here?"

"We don't know," said Maytig. "Leif says Tomi's been with the Swimmer, this time, longer than anyone ever was before. But we don't know what's happening. Tomi asked us not to talk to him."

"—Accelerating!" called one of the technicians at the instruments behind them.

Leif hissed shortly, in exasperation, between his teeth.

"There it goes," he said. "We'll lose it now."

Glancing into the tank, Johnny saw the imaged star-lights wheeling about the two figures.

"The Swimmer?" Johnny asked.

"It'll accelerate away and pass over, now. You'll see—"

Before the sentence was fully uttered, the Space Swimmer winked out without warning, like a blown candle flame. The lights came on in the tank and the starscape disappeared. In the tank Tomi lifted his head like someone starting awake, and turned to swim to the waterlock. A second later he emerged, dripping, onto the floor of the lab. He shoved the faceplate of his mask down on his chest.

"Any luck at all?" asked Leif, eagerly.

"He wouldn't talk to me," said Tomi thinly, automatically accepting the towel Maytig handed him. The boy was obviously furious, although he did not raise his voice.

"Wouldn't talk to you? You mean—he could have?" asked Leif, a little hesitantly. Looking at the man, Johnny was surprised to see that Leif as well as the other Lander technicians were staring at Tomi uncertainly.

For a second he could not understand what could be bothering them. And then he realized it was the appearance of Tomi's tightly contained fury. It must be more than a little upsetting to them to see a ten year old boy—even if he was a ten-year-old boy whose height and weight were nearly equal to their own—showing the cold, tight-lipped, controlled rage of an adult. They could not understand, as Maytig and the other sea-born could, that this boy had possessed the independence and responsibility of a grown man for four years now. And that in those years he had dealt with matters of life and death, for himself and others, as a routine daily occurrence.

"Of course he could have!" snapped Tomi. "But he just stayed there and watched me. He wouldn't answer. He's older than the Mugger—many times older. He's so old he—" The boy fumbled. "He's so old I can't say how old he is. That's why he wouldn't answer—and it's not because he's hungry like the Mugger either. He eats—sunlight—radiation, sort of. He just didn't want to talk to someone like me!"

"Well—" said Leif, wearily, "we'll try again—"

"Not with him!" snarled the boy. "He's too old." Tomi ceased suddenly to dry himself with the towel. His face smoothed out unexpectedly and became thoughtful. "We'll try a young one. One I can talk to . . ."

"Are you sure he heard you—this particular Space Swimmer, I mean?" asked Maytig.

He looked at her in surprise.

"Oh, yes," Tomi said.

"What did you say to him?" Johnny asked. Tomi transferred his gaze to his father.

"What you're supposed to say," he replied. "What I always said to the killer whales, and the seals, and like that. You know, from the *The Jungle Books*, The Master Word Baloo the bear taught Mowgli—'*We be of one blood, ye and I!*'"

The uneasy tension among the Lander technicians of Leif's crew, pricked into being by the unnatural sight of a grown man's fury in a boy, broke and found its relief in nervous laughter. Maytig turned and swept the gaze of her blue eyes among them, cutting short the merriment.

"Go to the clinic room," she said, giving Tomi a push. "They want to make some physical tests of you, after your experience with the Swimmer."

Tomi went off through the maze of equipment. Maytig turned to Johnny.

"Those Landers found us too easily," she said. "The Sea Captains were right. This combined lab is just too big to hide from their instruments."

"Yes," said Johnny soberly. He was more than certain in his own mind that the attack had been the "nudge" Stuve had promised him, if Johnny should be slow making up his mind to join forces with that Baron.

"But where can we go and be safe?" Maytig was saying in distress. "Where can we hide?"

Leif looked at her helplessly.

"Where we ought to have gone in the first place, of course," said Johnny. "Into space itself."

"Space?" echoed Maytig. She was staring at him. He saw they were all staring at him, and suddenly he remembered that in six years they could all have forgotten about the Academy ashore.

"The Space Academy in the Great Salt Desert of Utah still has its training ships," Johnny said. "You can't mothball a space-going vessel the way you can a navy surface ship. You have to keep them on standby power, or face the fact that six months' deterioration of the systems aboard her will leave you with a pile of junk. —And in the ex-Cadets, we've got men who've been trained to take such a ship from standby to full power, and off-world into space."

They still stared at him.

"But you can't steal a *spaceship!*" said Leif, at last, feebly.

"Of course we can," said Johnny.

# 13

The training spaceships of the Academy were powered by a fusion process for initial takeoff thrust, which ordinarily utilized several thousand tons of water pumped aboard for the purpose. However, the same mass of lead was kept stored aboard for emergency takeoffs. The lead was first broken down by excess solar temperatures and then utilized as the water would have been. Then, once outside the atmosphere, an ion drive would take over, because it was more economical of fuel.

Accordingly, all the requirements for lifting the spaceship were present even on standby conditions. Theoretically, the ship could take off as soon as the furnace breaking down the lead had reached its operating temperature—or in forty minutes from switch-on. But that was only theoretically. Accordingly, the men in underwater gear who, two weeks after the attack on the sea-lab, cut their way through the screen on the intake main supplying the Academy with water, and swam on into the Academy grounds—to flit later, one by one, through the nighttime darkness of the Academy spacefield and aboard one of the ships—made no attempt to raise the ship immediately. Instead they began a laborious and complete check of all equipment aboard.

There were twelve of them, counting Johnny. But the job was as huge as the vessel itself. Thirty-three hours passed; until, just after sundown on the Great Salt Desert, the ship suddenly spouted screaming blasts of superheated mass, and lifted slowly. It accelerated skyward, turning northward toward the Pole, and vanished in the direction of an escape orbit.

The air and space traffic instruments of the North American continent, unused to spaceship takeoffs these last six years, were caught flatfooted. Their instruments lost track of the ship somewhere over Victoria Island and two hundred miles up, while it was still plainly headed away from Earth.

—Nor did they pick it up, twelve hours later, when it slipped back into the Earth's atmosphere and descended softly down into the waters of the South Pacific, in an area where those waters were two miles deep above an undersea mountain range.

Here, fifty fathoms deep, the enormous ship was fitted with a magnetic envelope. With this to protect her against the pressures of the depths,

she descended the two miles of water to where she
was relatively safe from discovery by the Land.

Two weeks later, fitted inside with equipment
from the combined sea-and-Space-Swimmer-labs
she rose once more to the nighttime surface of the
ocean.

At the surface her takeoff processes were activated. She lifted from the waves into the night
sky; and headed out from the atmosphere and
gravity field of the planet in an escape orbit. The
instruments of air traffic ashore, on a land which
had decided sometime since that either fanatics or
fools had earlier stolen the ship and taken off to
lose themselves in unmapped space, paid little
attention to signs of its takeoff. Meteorites and
malfunctions often caused like signals.

Meanwhile, aboard the ship, the sea-born and
the technical crew headed by Leif headed outward from the sun roughly a hundred and twenty
million miles. This put them in orbit around the
sun halfway between the orbits of Earth and
Mars—at the inner edge of the solar system area
where Space Swimmers normally were to be
found. There followed a two-day period of testing
their equipment under space conditions.

Tomi fretted. He had long ago explored the
ship's every nook and cranny; and his sea-trained
body was unused to physical idleness. Johnny
finally found him an occupation by sending him
outside wearing a small ion-drive and the double
magnetic envelope that they were testing as a
spacesuit. Tommy was told to try it out and look
for bugs. There were no bugs and it was hard to
keep the boy from leaving the safe vicinity of the
spaceship. In all his life Tomi had never known

what it was to be lost. And the thought of being lost in space did not seem to register with him now as a possibility, in spite of warnings.

Meanwhile, the test of equipment under actual space conditions approached completion. Nothing remained but an attempt to put Tomi into actual space contact with a Swimmer.

"Well," said Leif, "let's look over what we have and what we've got to decide. —To start off with, we've got two necessary pieces of equipment. One, a pack of frozen oxygen with an adaptation of the waterlung that will furnish its wearer with five hours of breathable atmosphere. Two, a doubled magnetic envelope that will work, we hope, as a container for the atmosphere around Tomi and as a protection against harmful radiation. The radiation protection comes from the fact we can match the two envelopes to admit light only in the visible spectrum, in bearable quantities. By doubling the envelope, we produce a protective sandwich with a non-space-time condition between the joined faces of the two magnetic fields, one of each envelope. This ought to deflect any small space-born solid particles, or deflect the wearer from them, if their mass is too great."

He paused and looked at them both.

"That's the physical system," said Johnny. "But what about the interacting system—the human one?"

"That's it," said Leif. "It's your son that's going to be going out there, Johnny. According to theory and test, that doubled magnetic envelope should interact with the space roads—as Tomi calls them—along which the Swimmers move. Magnetically, the envelope duplicates the gas body of

the Swimmer. But we won't know until Tomi tries
it. —And we don't know what will happen if and
when it does interact."

"You told me," said Johnny, steadily, "—you
told me you believed Tomi would be able to move
along the roads with the Swimmers. That he
wouldn't need that ion drive he's wearing now."

"That's the theory," said Maytig. Her blue eyes
sought out Johnny's as if for justification, but he
kept his own gaze impersonal.

"The theory, yes," said Leif. "If it doesn't work,
no harm's done. —Nothing's accomplished,
either—" he smiled, his long face twisting wryly,
"—but no harm's been done. But if it works—
Tomi will have entered the web-system of magnetic forces we think exists all through the galaxy.
—If not through the universe. And what will happen to him then is anybody's guess."

"The point is," said Johnny. "You believe these
forces are in balance. You told me so."

"Yes, I did." Leif passed a lean hand over his
high forehead wearily. "The amount of electric
current flowing continuously in the interstellar
gas of our galaxy is estimated to be in the
neighborhood of 3,000,000,000,000,000,000 amperes. By contrast, a flash of terrestrial lightning
represents a flow of only around a hundred
thousand amperes. If a galactic magnetic field
representing an amperage like that estimated is to
be represented by the network of forces indiffer-
ent to ordinary physical laws of the Einsteinian
universe—such as we know exist in the special
magnetic fields of your irises and magnetic
envelopes—then that network *ought* to be in balance."

"Why?" challenged Maytig. "If it doesn't conform to other physical laws, why does it have to be balanced and stable?"

"Because," said Leif, with an effort, "it doesn't conform—but it coexists. I'd have to show it to you mathematically, and you wouldn't understand the mathematics. Just take my word for it. If the network of force lines—roads—didn't stay balanced, they'd collapse. Just like a house on Earth would collapse if there weren't internal forces holding it in shape."

"All right," said Johnny. "It balances. Then, what can happen to Tomi?"

"Nothing. But—" Leif checked himself. "What I mean is, we theorize that the Swimmers move along these lines of force, about this network, by creating minor imbalances in it. And while they're so moving they're essentially independent of ordinary space-time. So, for example, if a force line suddenly leaves this vicinity and continues (for reasons of necessary extra-special balance against other force lines) immediately at some point in space five hundred light-years away, the Swimmer leaves the spacial here and continues right along with the force line. To our spatially limited perception it looks as if he's jumped five hundred light-years of distance in no time at all. While, to him, he's just kept traveling at the same speed. The only thing is we theorize that—we don't know it."

Johnny shook his head.

"I don't follow you," he said.

"I mean," said Leif with great emphasis, "we really don't know—we don't know what happens when a Swimmer does what we call *passing over*.

Now, Tomi can go out there. We know now he can communicate with the younger Swimmers, and he can follow them in ordinary space-time with the ion drive. But"—Leif looked squarely at Johnny—"none of this'll do us any real good if he can't follow them the rest of the way—unless he passes over with them. And I repeat, we don't really know what will happen to him if he does."

"He tells me he'll have no trouble," said Johnny.

"Yes," said Maytig. Her face was unhappy. "But he's just a boy, after all. He's only ten years old. It's you who ought to decide."

"I'll decide when the moment comes," said Johnny. "Tomi's not going to go out alone, I've decided that much. I'll go with him. When it comes to the point where he faces passing over— then I'll decide and tell him what to do."

Two hours later, both father and son left the spaceship wearing their magnetic envelopes that were at once their spacesuits and space vehicles. Even to Johnny the sight of Tomi floating near him in the vacumn was a somewhat unnerving sight. At the same time it brought back the feeling of weightless freedom he had felt in the tank ashore. For within the magnetic envelopes neither of them wore anything but their ordinary sea-clothing of trunks or shorts. They were freer than birds had ever been. In the distant light of the sun, the faint rainbow-like halations of the double magnetic envelope about Tomi were invisible. He seemed to float there with only the atmosphere pack of frozen oxygen like a bulky packsack on his back to add to the appearance he would have presented in the sea-waters of Earth. Then the

little ion-drive in the base of the pack began to put out its near-invisible halo of blue gases and the illusion was spoiled.

Johnny touched the controls at his belt, beside the controls of the magnetic envelope. He felt the push of his own small ion-drive, and looking back, saw the spaceship in the distant sunlight, shrinking behind them. He looked ahead again and saw Tomi proceeding surely on, as if following some inner map.

Five minutes later, Tomi cut his drive and waved to Johnny to do likewise. Johnny was just behind the boy now, in apparently featureless space with the dark glove of star-lights all around them.

"There, Dad," said Tomi's voice over the radio circuit between the masks of their pack-connected waterlungs. "Feel it?"

Johnny frowned.

For a second he sensed nothing at all. And then, growing as he began to be aware of it, he began to feel something for which there were no words. It was as if some inner eye had suddenly become sensitive to the presence of a light his ordinary eyes could not perceive. He felt it—an illumination somehow almost like music, a vibration like the magnificent singing of a single violin sounding in his brain and bones and mind.

As he noticed it, it grew stronger. It seemed to gather him up with increasing power and carry him away with it. He was conscious of moving with increasing speed—although there was no external quality against which to measure this acceleration. For a moment he was puzzled by a feeling like a familiarity; as if he had touched this sensation somewhere else, before. And then recognition came to him.

He had, indeed, felt it before. It was the same sort of inner, non-physical sensation that was part of his third-generation sea-born sense of location and direction in the waters of the deep oceans. That sense that sounded in him whenever he had come into one of the great currents of the sea. The particular, individual, recognized feel of the Liman Current, as opposed to the Gulf Stream, the Labrador Current, or the Kuroshio. Like these, this present feeling was the sudden inner recognition of power, and balancing movement and direction. The awareness of a development in movement that extended to unguessed distances, all of which were perceptible and related to this present place. But the sea-feeling compared to this had been like the chirping of a sparrow to the song of the nightingale.

"There, Dad!" shouted Tomi's voice, suddenly over the radio circuit. "There's one of them now!"

Johnny turned his head to look about him—and there, still as small as a handkerchief seen at a distance across a wide room, was the shape of a Space Swimmer, blue in the distant sunlight. Johnny turned back to look at Tomi and saw that the boy was no longer in front of him.

Tomi was off to the right, moving away at an angle that was directed at the angle of movement of the still distant, undulating blue shape of the Swimmer.

"Tomi!" called Johnny over the mask radio.

Distantly, he saw the boy's head turn and search him out. In the trickery of vision peculiar to featureless space, Tomi did not look far off, but rather dwindled in size until he was hardly larger than Johnny's hand. The sunlight gleamed on the semi-transparent magnetic envelope, evoking a sudden burst of rainbow colors from it. He saw the envelope was undulating as the bodies of the Swimmers undulated as if to the current Johnny himself still felt coursing through him.

He looked about him. His own envelope undulated also.

"How do I get over where you are?" asked Johnny over the radio, turning his attention back to Tomi.

"Feel for another road, Dad," said Tomi's voice in the mask receiver. "They're all around. Just feel. You'll find it!"

Johnny half-closed his eyes and tried to give himself over completely to the feeling inside him. For a long moment there was no perceptible change. Then he thought of the feeling of the ocean currents again, and all the deep inner touch of the sea. For a moment his perceptions fumbled with what he searched after . . . and then something seemed to slip inside him. He felt—saw— experienced—there was no small human word for it—the road on which he traveled, like a glowing strip of light through the star-strewn space.

It was like the first experience of tunnel vision to a man long blind. He seemed to look far out along a narrow way, and—as he looked closer, he saw more. Not only the one singing road he followed, but a studding of intersections with crossing roads at all angles. Gradually his vision widened. It was not a tunnel but an expanding globe he looked into. The pieces of other roads intersected in all dimensions. There was a difference in their brightness. Some glowed strongly, some more faintly. And, in the distance, as they faded out on either side, there was a hint of fuzziness, a ghost, a mist of other lines—even more fine-drawn yet and leading farther.

A new recognition plucked at Johnny's mind. There was another familiarity about this. Something there—and yet not there—something almost understood—

"*Dad!*"

It was Tomi's voice over the radio circuit. Johnny's attention came back to his son with a jerk. The boy was closer now, just above the Swimmer's blue form, coming back at an angle that would bring them across some little distance below Johnny but both of them were accelerating rapidly.

"I've got to go with him. I've got to pass over if I'm going to stay with him, Dad!" shouted Tomi over the radio. "He's one of the young ones. He wants to show me something. It's all right. I'll meet you back at the ship. Is it all right? I've got to pass over in just a second—"

Johnny hesitated. Tomi and the Swimmer were rushing upon and below him now. The moment of decision was at hand. The face of Tomi's dead mother rose in his mind and at the same time with one great stride forward the causative pattern brought the possibilities of the world's future to bear upon this same second. His heart moved in his chest. Instinctively he reached out as he would in the sea—to feel the singing current on which he traveled, to see if it was all right. And the answer that rang back inside him was reassuring.

"Go!" said Johnny.

Almost in the same second, Swimmer and boy winked out together. Johnny's new inner perception saw them vanish in an impression of red light—like a soft flaring of the lighted road upon which Johnny himself had been traveling all this time.

And then there was nothing but empty void and the stars.

Johnny hung alone in space. Suddenly as it had come upon him, his perception of the space roads was fading. Even as he noticed the fact, they dwindled to silence and darkness and were gone.

As Tomi had gone—with the Swimmer—into limitless space.

A dullness, a heavy, earth-bound feeling began to seep back into Johnny, deadening all his senses, making him feel numb and spiritless. It was a feeling such as an eagle would feel after flight, to be shackled and weighed with heavy chains to the drab earth, away from the freedom of blue sky.

He spoke into the radio circuit of his mask.

"Leif?" he said. "Leif, were you monitoring?"

Leif's voice came back, weakly and interspersed with static, as if from some distance.

"We were listening. Did Tomi pass over, then?"

"Yes," said Johnny, dully. "I'm out here somewhere by myself. Take a fix on my transmitter and come and get me, will you?"

"We'll move the ship to you," said Leif. "So Tomi can return to the spot he passed over from, and find us. Sit tight."

The transmission from Leif's end ceased. Johnny hung in space, waiting. After a while a distant winking of light caught his attention. It was the sun-glitter on the approaching spaceship. It swelled slowly in size toward him until at last it loomed enormously beside him, blotting out the stars. The air-lock opened. He activated his ion-drive and jetted slowly inside the ship.

After that came the waiting. The snail-slow minutes crept by and grew into hours and Tomi did not reappear. The hours of the five-hour supply of frozen oxygen in his pack dragged themselves wearily past with the exhausted slowness of one of the great female sea-turtles returning to the sea after laying her eggs far above high tide on some sandy beach. Johnny was sitting in the monitoring room of the ship, watching the resonance screen which would light up with a dot of illumination if Tomi's magnetic envelope should reappear anywhere within a radius of a hundred thousand miles of the ship.

He felt a touch on his shoulder and looked up to see Maytig standing over him.

"Pat's calling," Maytig said, "by orbital relay from the Entertainment Estates in Australia."

Johnny got up and followed her into the communications section of the ship. Pat's lean face looked out at him from the communications screen there. It was hard for Johnny to think of that face being carried piggy-back on a tight laser beam all the way from Earth so that only a few seconds separated Pat and himself in this moment. Right now Earth and its problems seemed at the other end of the universe from this waiting ship.

"Hello, Pat," said Johnny.

"Sorry to bother you. They tell me you're waiting for Tomi," said Pat. He was speaking in the tongue-and-nail clicking of the dolphin code. His eyes met Johnny's for a second in a look of understanding. "But you're needed back here on surface. Use the code when you answer me. There's no way to keep this relay from being snooped."

"All right," answered Johnny, in the code, "What's up?"

"Stuve's made his move," said Pat. "He's accused all the rest of the Barons of being in on a plot to divide up the world into private kingdoms."

"That's not much of a move," said Johnny, staring at Pat's face in the screen. "I can't see the Landers getting excited about that. Even if the Barons did plot to set up private kingdoms, how'd they force all the people ashore to agree to be subjects in their kingdoms? They've got only a handful of retainers, apiece, to force their will on the Landers."

"Not according to Stuve," clicked Pat. "They've got us." His eyes met Johnny's, grimly. "Stuve claims that there's more than a billion of us in the sea, that we've been training and arming for six years to take over the land; and that Ebberly's made a deal with us to act as policemen of the Land in the Barons' new kingdoms, with the other Landers as serfs. And the Land believes him— they're half in riot, half in panic ashore, with the other Barons holed up at Ebberly's Estates North. Ebberly wants you to come there, right away, from wherever you are."

"I can't come right away," said Johnny. "In an hour-and-a-half Tomi's air runs out—" He broke off. "It won't be much longer than that. Tell Ebberly so."

The screen darkened on Pat's nod.

Johnny and the rest aboard ship went back to the painful process of waiting. Half an hour, an hour, an hour and ten minutes went by . . . . Then, abruptly, an hour and twenty some minutes after Pat's call, less than ten minutes before Tomi's oxygen pack would have been exhausted, the boy's happy voice hailed the ship over the radio circuit as he appeared just outside its air-lock. Beside him were three Space Swimmers, one red, one reddish-orange and one green. Big as the training spaceship was, they dwarfed it like crows descending on a fallen ear of corn.

The air-lock was opened, and Tomi came bursting aboard through its inner door to start talking at once to the crowd gathered in the ready room and waiting for him there.

"They're young ones," he began the moment his mask was off. He clambered out of his exhausted oxygen pack and equipment, still talking. "I made friends with them all right."

"Where did you go?" Leif demanded.

"They took me all over. I've seen all sorts of suns. Planets too. Some with blue on them, and oceans like Earth—we couldn't get too close. You know how it is with an eddy in the water how it sucks you down? It's the same way with planets or suns, or any solid body in space to the Swimmers—" He broke off suddenly as a vibration through the body of the ship announced the starting of the ion-drive. In the screen beside the air-lock, the three shapes of the Swimmers could be seen dwindling back from them. "Where're we going? Are we going home?"

"Yes," said Johnny. "Something's come up.

You didn't have any trouble passing over?"

"No." Tomi shook his head. "But I don't know how I do it. It just sort of happens when you get going in the right direction."

"Did you ask your friends—the Swimmers?" said Leif. "Do they know?"

Johnny and all of them waited for the answer.

Tomi looked at the balding man. "I'm sorry," he said, "that's what I was going to tell you. They don't know. You see they're real old, but they're young. I mean they've lived a long time but to them they're young. One of them told me he remembers when there wasn't any ice at our South Pole. But they aren't like us. When they're born they're just barely alive—like clams. Then, gradually they grow up until they're like animals, then finally they get so they think like people. But they live almost forever and it takes a long time. My friends couldn't understand me being born with brains to start with."

"You mean—?" Leif broke off, turning to Maytig. "That makes sense, come to think of it. There's nothing to kill them out here in space. They could live forever as Tomi says. They could start life as merely clouds of living gas and individually evolve into thinking creatures. But that's tremendous!" Leif said, turning back to Tomi. "If the young ones you know have developed this far—how much farther the older ones must have developed. Think what they can teach us! Tomi, next time you've got to get to talk to one of the older Swimmers."

"But that's what I told you back in the tank!" said the boy.

Leif and the rest stared at him.

"Told me?" said Leif. "What?"

"The old ones won't talk," said Tomi. "Remember how I told you the old one I met the first time in the tank wouldn't talk to me? My friends—the young ones—say it isn't just me, or us. The old ones won't even talk to them."

Leif and Maytig looked at each other.

"Maybe," suggested Maytig, "the older Swimmers *can't* talk."

"Oh, they can talk," said Tomi. "They can tell you to leave them alone. And they know things all right—like how the passing over works. My friends say they know almost everything. And you can feel it's true—somehow—when you get close to an old one. But they won't tell any of it."

He looked around at the ring of adult faces.

"It's like—like something they believe in," said Tomi. "That's why they let the Space Academy kill them when the Academy used to capture them the way you said, Dad. The old ones know but they'll never tell. They'd rather die first!" He looked directly at Johnny. "I'm sorry," he said. "I'm sorry, Dad, but that's the way they are."

# 14

It was just before dawn, fourteen hours later, that the spaceship came down over a cloud-covered North Atlantic and sank itself forty fathoms below the waves until the attachment of air-filled pods balanced it in the water beside the Headquarters Home of the North Atlantic Area of the sea-People. Leaving the ship for the Home, Johnny found a smallboat waiting to take him ashore, and also most of the Sea Captains, already gathered in expectation of a showdown with the Land. Most of the fighting men of the third generation in the North Atlantic Area were either approaching or within fifty miles of the Savannah Stand shoreline now. They had begun to gather the moment Pat had called the sea to warn them he was calling back Johnny at Ebberly's request.

In that fifty-mile radius area now, the Sea Cap-

tains told Johnny, were better than twenty
thousand armed men ready to move if Johnny
gave the word. Other forces were gathering in the
other sea areas. Or, the total sea population could
retreat to ocean deeps within two hours, in case
the ultimate action to start destruction of the continents by initiating deep-sea geologic disturb-
ances was ordered.

Johnny shook his head.

"I've still got hopes of pulling out a solution—
for us and the Land, both." He saw Leif listening
and staring at him as he said this, and he looked
back, evenly and deliberately. The land-born scientist dropped his eyes. "If anything happens to
me, you're on your own. But talk with the Land.
Give them one more chance before you fire off
your nuclear charges and wake up the Ring of
Fire."

He swung his eyes around the half-circle of
third-generation faces.

"You'll do that?" he said. "I can count on you to
talk first?"

They nodded. He turned and went to his waiting smallboat.

There was no one on the landing stairs above
the ducted flyer stand. And the flyers themselves
sat in their ranks, lifeless and unmoving.

Johnny left the smallboat, which turned back
into the sea, and stepped onto the first concrete
level of the steps. He ran lightly up them and
stepped in through the irises of the entrance doors
into the Terminal.

It was empty.

Lights glowed, signs glittered and moved above

restaurant and bar areas. But in all that vast, towering-walled enclosure, no figure moved. But one.

As Johnny walked rapidly into the area of the main floor, a tall, lean shape rode to the bottom of the ramp from the mezzanine area of the air-shuttle buses, and strode toward him. Even at this distance, Johnny saw it was Pat. He walked rapidly toward Pat, and they met perhaps fifty yards in front of the foot of the ramp.

"I've got a private ship waiting for you on the air-shuttle area," said Pat. "Come on. The Civil Group's arresting anyone who moves in the Chicago Complex area. You'd never get through there by subway to Ebberly's Estates North."

He turned about and began to head back toward the ramp. Johnny went with him. Their long legs made short work of the distance to the ramp and up it. Sitting in among the air-shuttle bus area was the stubby, powerful shape of a small private rocket ship. Pat jerked open the door and gestured Johnny in, then slid in behind Johnny to take the other seat facing the controls.

A second later the door closed, the rocket jerked skyward, driving for altitude beyond the air traffic controlled area.

"So the Groups are ready to fight each other, at last?" said Johnny.

"At last—yes," said Pat. His thin face was set in harsh lines and looked older than Johnny could remember seeing it look before. "Most of the rank and file of the Civil Group think the Barons—except Stuve—are trying to dissolve it so that they can take over management of the world."

He leveled the ship off, finally. Below them the

land was featureless and the horizon line was faintly curved. Above, the sky was black with the stars faintly showing, though it was broad daylight. Ahead, Johnny could see the sprawl of the Great Lakes.

"How'd it start?" asked Johnny.

Pat began to turn the ship back toward the surface of the planet again.

"Last night—early last night," he said. "Men wearing Transportation Marks and livery kidnaped Gino Morandi"—he glanced sideways at Johnny—"the Civil Group Baron. Maybe you remember—?"

"I remember," said Johnny. "Go on. Have they found him, yet?"

"They found his body this morning. But an hour after the kidnapping was announced on the News Services, yesterday, Stuve went on the air to announce that he had been approached to join a conspiracy, but turned it down. He claimed Ebberly and the five other largest Barons had conspired to kill Morandi and dissolve the Civil Group."

"Which would dissolve civil law, ashore?"

"That's right," Pat nodded. They were descending at a sharp angle into the atmosphere now; and a corner of the screen viewing the area between Lake Michigan and Lake Superior below them showed a corner of one stubby wing glowing cherry-red with the air friction. "With no civil law, the people in the large Groups would have the protection of their own outfits. But most of the world would be unorganized, defenseless, and without anyone to turn to for policing and justice."

They were coming down and a moment later they landed at the private rocket pad of Ebberly's Transportation Estates North. Pat led Johnny past the armed men guarding the pad onto a walkway that carried them back to that same lakeside pavilion Johnny had now entered twice before.

Inside the pavilion, Pat led him to the same room, half office, half lounge, where he had had those two previous interviews with Ebberly. As before, Ebberly was there now but this time there were others with him.

"You heard," Ebberly was saying to these others as Pat and Johnny came in. Ebberly stood with his back to the entrance and the two sea-born as they came through it. He stood with legs spread apart, shoulders squared, staring down at five other Barons seated in a rough semicircle behind the desk Ebberly himself was in the habit of occupying. He did not look particularly disturbed or unhappy. Beside him Johnny recognized Quayle Walser, the thin sixty year old who headed the Communications Group, on the left. Next to him were thick-bodied, middle-aged Pao Jacoski of Fabrication, then fat, old Wally Kutch of Supply, Michael Under of Clerical, and then Ed Poira of Distribution, a man almost as tough-looking as Kai Ebberly himself. "—The latest word," Ebberly went on, "is that Stuve's calling for a plebescite. For a world-wide government. The very thing our Groups have fought to get away from for a hundred years. You know who the head of that Government would be—Barth Stuve."

Ebberly paused, put his hands together behind his back, and cracked the knuckles of his first and second fingers on his left hand, deliberately, one

after the other. The sound and action in the face of
the silence of the other Barons brought a feeling of
savage and contemptuous power into the taut air
of the room.

Johnny walked forward, followed by Pat, and at
the sound of footsteps Ebberly turned around.

"Here you are," he said, as they stopped in front
of him. His eyes met Johnny's squarely.

"Yes," said Johnny. Ebberly's face, he saw, was
calm and the tones of his voice were reasonable.

"Well, Joya," said Ebberly, evenly, "you were
right and I was wrong. Would you like me to
apologize—eat crow? I'll be glad to. Because we
need you now."

"I'm not so sure about that," said Ed Poira, his
hard, thick-fleshed face unfriendly.

"You're a fool, Ed," said Ebberly, without rais-
ing his voice or taking his gaze off Johnny. "You
always were. When Stuve suggested outlawing
these people, you were the first one to go along
with it."

"You went along, too," growled Poira.

"And I was a fool, too," said Ebberly. He turned
to Johnny. "Well, Joya, how about it? If Stuve gets
control of the world, there's an end to progress.
There's an end to any hope of a future way to the
stars. And that's what I want. So I'm willing to pay
any price to keep Stuve from getting control. And
so, too, should you people in the sea be willing to
pay any price. Because if he gets control he's not
going to let any group of people exist that aren't
under his control. And that means the end of your
sea-culture, too."

He stopped. Johnny said nothing.

"You want me to do all the talking?" said Ebberly. "All right. Barth Stuve is holed up in his Rocky Mountain hunting lodge. It's on top of a mountain above Yellowstone Park. The only way to stop him is to go in and get him—only we can't, because the place is a fortress. It's got space-and-atmosphere defenses against anything from missiles to kamikaze pilots; and the mountainside is too rugged to get heavy weapons up close enough to do any good. Besides, all our retainers put together aren't enough to take the place by frontal assault up the slopes. We can't get at Barth—but you can."

He stopped to look at Johnny significantly.

"Go on," said Johnny.

"There's a deep lake inside his walls on the mountain top," said Ebberly. "And a river that comes out of the side of the mountain a distance lower down. The river is fed by the lake, through a series of caves inside the mountain. There's a way in up that river. It'd be half underwater work and half cave-climbing, and no men we've got could do it—but you people could. And a force of your men could come up right inside Barth's defenses."

Johnny nodded slowly.

"I thought something like that," he said. "But why do you think I'd spend the lives of my people just to haul your chestnuts out of the fire?"

"We'll give you anything you ask for if you do," said Ebberly. "My word on it."

"Keep your word for someone who believes in it," said Johnny. He looked at all the Barons grimly. "All right—here's our price for getting Barth for you. An admission that the original outlawing of the sea-People was unjust. And a guarantee that the seas will belong to us, as national territory—not only the under-seas, but the surface of them, and the atmosphere over them."

Ebberly stared back at him for a second without expression.

"All right," he said, then, calmly. "I agree. Get going."

"Not just yet," said Johnny. "First, I want all of you here to issue a joint statement to the news services, right now, announcing the revocation of the decree of outlawry, and the guarantee that the seas will be ours." He looked past Ebberly at the other Barons. "Do that—and I'll save your necks. Otherwise, I won't."

"Never mind them," said Ebberly harshly. "They'll do it. I promise. We'll make the announcement right now." He turned to the other Barons.

Johnny himself turned to Pat.

"Pat," he said. "Get a message to the Sea Captains and have them send—" He broke off, turning to Ebberly. "How many men has Stuve got on that mountain top?"

"Maybe a hundred—it's not that big," said Ebberly.

"Get fifty men—ex-Cadets by preference," said Johnny, turning back to Pat. "Maybe you better go get them yourself, come to think of it."

"No," said Pat, looking steadily back at him. "I'll message. When you go after Barth Stuve, I'm going with you."

# 15

It was five o'clock Mountain Time when Johnny, with Pat and the fifty sea-born fighting men, landed on a snowy slope in the Rockies. Less than a thousand feet above was the rocky crest that held the hunting lodge of Stuve in a cup-shaped depression below the peak. The peak was not so high that pines and spruce were not thick on the slope and in the cup. And the cup had high walls of the natural rock surrounding it on all sides but one. In this one gap was the Terminal for the area.

Johnny led Pat and the fifty sea-born up the wind-packed snow of the slope between the pine trees. The cloudless sky overhead was warm with a freakishly early breath of false spring. A hawk circled overhead. Far across the gulf of open air behind them was the curve of the Gallatin Range, beneath which lay Yellowstone Park.

Back at Transportation Estates North, Johnny had examined air photos of the rocky cup and the lodge within it. The cup was more than a mile in diameter. The inner half of this space was taken up by a blue and deep mountain lake, well-stocked with trout warmly unfrozen beneath the weather shield that protected everything in the cup. There was nothing to hunt under that shield but the trout and some imported, rare albino squirrels with enormously fluffy and decorative tails. These inhabited the pine- and fir-treed shores, which in a nearly natural state ran down in the form of slopes, deep in brown fallen pine needles, to the water's edge. Except where these trees had been cleared to make room for the lodge.

The spacious lodge itself ran down the slope toward the lake from the entrance. Its final structure was a tower which lifted at last on the very lakeshore, the curve of its outer side bulging out over the water. A tower four-stories high with two balconies projecting from the upper two stories on the land side. There were no windows, and there could be no fixed weapons in the tower. The rest of the lodge was also windowless, its walls armored against missile weapons and magnetically screened against any power that could be carried against it in the form of individually portable sonic or electronic weapons. The one soft spot, Johnny had decided, was the back part of the entrance Terminal, just inside the mountain gap of the entrance to the area. If he and the sea-born could break in there, then they could fight their way down the lodge from the inside.

Now, they reached the spot, guarded by some of the Ebberly's retainers, where the underground stream broke from the mountainside. One by one, the sea-born men slipped masks up over their faces and took to the water. The current was difficult, but they had come equipped with belt jet units; and with these they slipped into the interior of the mountain along the riverbed like salmon working upstream.

Within the mountain the river proceeded by a series of cave-born falls and rapids. The route was a slow one, but not difficult for anyone but a Lander. Only a little less than an hour later, they cut their way with torches through a too-narrow stone entrance into the lake above, only some twenty feet below the surface and a dozen feet out from the shore.

The shore itself was overhung thickly by brush and tree-tangles. They slipped ashore under this cover and circled through the woods around to the three-story-tall, plaster-white, back wall of the Terminal entrance. Johnny raised his hand in signal for the attack.

The sullen sound of the explosion of the sonic bomb lobbed by the advance party to blow open the Terminal's three-story-tall, plaster-white, outside gate, jarred on Johnny, when he with Pat and the advance guard of the sea-born were still fifty feet down from it. The sound and the sudden pressure of air reminded him of the raid on New York Complex six years before when he had led the expedition to rescue the ex-Cadets held prisoner by the Land. He broke into a run now, abandoning concealment, scrambling up and forward.

The Terminal entrance was blown clear and open when he reached it. A blast of warm air was blowing out of it. A few metal scraps of wreckage, a few bodies, black against the white snow, and shards of broken gate were all that they saw. Then they were into the Terminal, the ex-Cadets behind Johnny spreading out with sonic rifles in their hands to take advantage of their cover. Their original training at the Academy had been improved by six years of being hunted. They moved like professional soldiers. It was the difference between wolf and dog with them and the hired toughs in livery that made up the force backing them up.

Also they were now all caught up in their third-generation sense of location and the awareness of each others' position. They moved forward with a sureness no land-born fighters could have felt, and the pale beams of the visual-sighting mechanisms of their rifles began to trace paths through the air between the crowded trees before them.

They were all down on their bellies now and wriggling forward. Pat, in spite of his long time ashore, was keeping up at Johnny's side.

He and Johnny were in the front line of crawling attackers and they had come within thirty yards of the inner entrance to the main lodge building. Johnny paused to click a command in dolphin code with his tongue. His throat mike picked it up and carried it to the sea-born off to his right. Fifty feet away, a sonic bomb was lobbed in toward the now closed entrance doors before him.

The bomb was triggered by a magnetic shield at a six-foot distance beyond the doors. But the backwash of its premature explosion made the building wall sag, and slammed the sea-born in the front rank back hard against the concrete terminal floor.

"Now!" shouted Johnny into his throat mike to the men behind him.

He got to his feet and charged the building. He could feel the presence of the sea-born all around him and could see Patrick beside him. There was a sonic explosion dead ahead, inside the area of the magnetic shield. They were through the shield then. A door, sagging on its pivot, was before Johnny.

He burst through into darkness—felt, rather than saw, sighting beams of pale light winking at him and went down flat. Pat, he discovered, was beside him on a carpeted floor, sonic rifle cuddled to a lean cheek. In the interior gloom, Pat's face seemed washed of its lines—seemed almost as young as Johnny remembered it from their days in the sea together before even the Space Academy had been built. The lean fingers that had written and played the music of the People of the Sea were curled and steady about the rifle. It was Pat's six-year-old sense of guilt that had brought him to this place; Johnny understood that. But—he should not be here, thought Johnny suddenly. Any of the rest of us but not Pat. No hired gunman of the Land should be allowed to cut the thread of that vital music still unwritten in Pat's mind, and stretching into the future. Yet he had insisted on coming and the Sea held that every man's life was in his own hands. I must try to get him through this alive, somehow, thought Johnny.

The room was cleared now of defenders.

"All right, Pat?" Johnny asked.

"All right," said Pat.

They came to their feet in a crouch and scurried forward with others of the sea-born felt behind them. Abruptly they broke through an electronic light baffle into brilliant illumination. They were on top of a group of five men wearing Construction livery and the mark of compass-and-bob on their white, short-sleeved shirts. The men were aiming a thermite thrower. Johnny and Pat crashed into them without stopping and things dissolved into a hand-to-hand struggle in which the physically superior and more wolfish-minded sea-born brought them quickly under control. Johnny stood up and saw that he was surrounded by members of his own attacking force, and that they were at the end of a long, brightly-lit corridor.

They raced for the double doors at the end of the corridor, fought a brief battle with their rifles with whoever was behind the doors, and broke them down on top of a sprawl of dead bodies. They found themselves in a large room surrounding a swimming pool of Olympic proportions. A steam explosion triggered off from water in the pool drove them back for a second, and then they were running forward around the edges of the pool toward a wall of French windows beyond.

Pat was still at Johnny's side.

Three rooms of fighting later, something in Johnny cried sudden warning. He flung himself aside and the whole mountain on which the building rested seemed to rear upwards and tear itself out by the roots. There was a moment of dust and roaring sound, and then nothing. Johnny opened his eyes and clambered to his feet. The

dust was thinning. About him, as he turned his
head, he saw that all the walls had disappeared.
Everything was suddenly, deathly still.

The bodies of Stuve's men and the bodies of two
of the sea-born were strewn about, their mouths
bloody from the internal rupture of the sonic explosion that had just engulfed them. They lay in a
pattern on the ground, like a flower pattern of
which Johnny was the focal point. He gazed at it
and recognized finally the causative calculation
in the split second that had saved him. He had
leaped to the small dead spot at the very center of
a sonic explosion. He looked for Pat and tried to
remember if Pat had still been with him before the
explosion. But he could not remember, and
among the bodies Pat was not to be seen.

Johnny shook his head to clear it. He felt dazed.
And although the enemy's distorter had ceased its
buzzing—that was set up to distort the bounce-
echo sighting of the rifles where the sighting
beams were useless—his ears continued to ring
with its sound. He looked around. The building
about him had utterly ceased to exist. Instead, an
open gap now separated the part of its structure
behind him from the last part of the structure
before the four-story tower swelling out over the
water, on the lake edge.

It seemed as if no time at all had passed, but
Johnny saw now that the sun was almost down to
the sharp-toothed horizon of the mountain peaks.
Its level rays were red as the blood on the mouths
of the dead around him, and their light partially
blinded him. Or so he thought, and then he saw
the light was striking a reflection into his eyes
from a shimmering coating about the tower. He

blinked and looked closer and saw a magnetic shield standing out only a few inches from the round wall and running up the towerside to curve out for only a foot or so beyond the third- and fourth-story balconies and the exterior staircase that ran between them and down to the ground outside the tower.

A door in the base of the tower, exposed by the explosion, was firmly closed behind the magnetic shield. The foot of the outside staircase, too, was enclosed behind the shield. Although that shield would not stop their physical passage through the door, while it existed their sonic and vibratory rifles and other weapons could not harm the tower. Johnny looked back behind him and spoke into his throat mike.

"Somebody see if they can find me a phone in the building still standing back there."

There was a moment's wait, and then one of the sea-born came up with a small, mother-of-pearl pyramid. Johnny took it and touched the peak of the pyramid with the tip of his forefinger.

"Information?" he said.

There was a second's pause, then a silvery voice answered.

"This is Information."

"Yes," said Johnny. "I want the phone number of the west-end tower of a hunting lodge belonging to the Control Group. I'm in a different part of the lodge myself, at the moment. Would you check back, locate, and connect me?"

"That number you wish may be restricted, sir."

"If it is," said Johnny, "please check with the party there at the moment. I have reason to believe they'll speak to me."

He held the phone and waited for the results. As he waited he turned to the nearest of the sea-born among the armed men surrounding him in the waiting silence since the explosion.

"Have you seen Pat?" he asked.

"Your cousin, Johnny?" asked the other. "No, I haven't seen him since we got into the building."

"Would you see if you can find him, back along the way?" Johnny asked. The man turned and went. Johnny turned to another standing nearby.

"Get back down the outside to our transportation ships on the mountainside," said Johnny. "Fly down to the nearest Transportation Center—Yellowstone Park must have one—and call Ebberly. Get permission to bring back equipment heavy enough to blow the magnetic shield about this tower."

"Your party, sir."

"Hello, Johnny," said the soft, baritone voice of Barth Stuve. "I've been expecting you to call. I'm willing to surrender—of course, on my own terms."

"What are they?" Johnny asked.

"Come on in alone and I'll tell you," Stuve answered. "Alone and unarmed. I'm alone in here myself. Do you believe me?"

"It doesn't matter if I do or not," said Johnny. "I'll come in."

He laid his sonic rifle on the ground and dropped his side-arm beside it. He looked at the stairs running up to the two balconies and then at the door in the base of the tower. The door swung inward, opening before him. There was only darkness behind it.

He went toward it and the magnetic screen

plucked at him like the film of a soap bubble, as he passed through. He stepped into the darkness and the door swung to click shut behind him.

Lights went on around him. He found himself in a circular room furnished like a lounge. A noiselessly running escalator ramp mounted and descended in the center of the room, disappearing up through the ceiling overhead.

He took the up-ramp to the floor above, which seemed to be a suite of offices, empty. He continued on to the next floor and passed through a large dining room, also deserted. Above that was a lounge, and on the fourth level he found himself in the middle of a small central hallway with a door to either side, closed and silent.

"Left-hand door," said Stuve's voice from somewhere about the hallway walls.

Johnny turned to and touched the left-hand door. It opened before him and he could see what seemed to be a walnut-paneled study furnished in the style of the late nineteenth century. A heavy red carpet with oriental figures was positioned in the center of the floor, leaving only a rim of polished wood flooring between its edges and the walls. An old-fashioned fireplace occupied a central position in the wall to Johnny's right, with a single slab of maple-sugar brown marble for a mantelpiece. Right now the whole room was gilded with sunset light from the false-window, a vision screen in the wall directly opposite the door where Johnny had entered. This wall curved outward to fit the curve of the tower and the screen in its center showed the peaceful, darkening waters of the lake below the setting sun.

Beyond the fireplace at the end of the room, and

before the window, was a solid-fronted desk behind which, in a gray-furred jacket of arctic wolf, Stuve was standing. The ridiculously wide shoulders of the jacket obstructed the view of the peaceful lake waters. Johnny walked up to the desk and stopped in front of it.

For a second he and Stuve merely looked at each other across its bare, hard-polished surface.

"So you came to hear my terms," said Stuve, softly.

"That's right," said Johnny.

"I don't think so," said Stuve. He had been standing with both hands hanging down out of sight behind the desk. He lifted his right hand now and there was a sonic pistol in it. "You came in here, like a sensible man, to kill me."

"No," said Johnny. "Not if you give up. Not if you withdraw from trying to control things." At the sight of the sonic pistol a cold feeling had stirred at the base of his neck, and now his mind switched into the cool lightning of its highest gear, examining the room about the two of them. He reminded himself that Stuve's mind would be working with a like swiftness and there was not the usual advantage to be depended upon.

"No," said Stuve. "But you know I won't. I'm disappointed. I thought you'd be more honest with me. I am with you. I got you in here to kill you—since you wouldn't accept my earlier offer of partnership. Look—"

He walked out from behind the desk, keeping the pistol steady on Johnny. He moved to the near end of the mantle-piece, reached up and touched it, pushing outward against it.

The mantlepiece corner moved and clicked.

The whole fireplace swung back, pivoting on its far corner, revealing a smooth, circular shaft walled in shining metal. A metal ladder led down it toward a light that beat upward from below.

"I wanted you to understand, and see this before I killed you, Johnny," he said. "This was my escape hatch, all along. By the time your men outside blow their way in here, I'll be down there and on a private subway line leading to the Yellowstone Park Terminal."

He paused, staring at Johnny. Johnny tensed himself.

"It's your last chance to change your mind," he said. "I waited here for you in this lodge, knowing you'd be leading the attackers, knowing you'd come in here. I wanted to save you if you could be—"

His eyes narrowed. Johnny saw his own teasing had been noticed at last. He flung himself forward, both hands chopping inward like the blades of a scissors—his left hand slapping against the barrel of the sonic pistol, his right hand striking like an axe-blade against Stuve's wrist. The pistol flew against the far wall of the room. And at the same time Johnny whipped his left hand back again across his body, chopping up and back-edged at Stuve's throat.

But the advantage in sea-born reflexes he had counted on to disarm Stuve—for he had foreseen the pistol, otherwise he would have never risked himself in here—was not enough to do this additional job for Johnny. Stuve's throat was not there. Stuve had leaped back at the same instant that the pistol was knocked from his grasp and the corner of the desk now separated him from Johnny.

Johnny made a sudden grab, but his fingers closed only on a handful of Stuve's fur jacket and the shirt beneath. Together jacket and shirt ripped apart as Stuve leaped back once more with an alertness that showed that the lightning of his own thoughts had calculated Johnny's grab. In the sunset coming from the false window he stood with the shreds of his jacket and shirt falling about his waist. And he said nothing, only drew in his breath with a faint hiss between his teeth. His hands rested lightly on the surface of the desk and his eyes glittered in his white, still face.

Johnny stood crouched slightly—checking and reassessing the situation at the sight of Stuve's upper body. The fur jackets with their bulging, padded shoulders that the other man wore had seemed to the world, and Johnny as well, to be a ridiculous improvement on fashion. Now Johnny remembered the thick brown mustache on the upper lip of Stuve's cousin, one of the Hunters who had attacked the berg-Home when Pat and Maytig came. The mustache, Pat had told him then, had hidden a deformed upper lip on the face of Stuve's cousin. The jackets, Johnny saw now, had been a clever trick to hide the shape and size of the deformed shoulders of Stuve.

Those shoulders were not merely unusual, they were frightening. Their width would have suited a man no less than seven feet in height. But they did not possess the weight of flesh and muscle that should have gone with that expanse of skeleton bone. They were like the shoulders of a starved giant.

By compensation, or perhaps by unrelenting exercise, the arms below the shoulderpoints, however, swelled and bulged with knotted muscle. The muscles were not thick as the muscles of a weight lifter might have been, but they were so etched in strength beneath the tight, smooth skin that they might have been modeled for anatomical study. Instinct, seeing those strange and corded muscles, triggered the calculations of Johnny's swiftly-moving mind and decided him to avoid them. He had been about to reach across the desk once more in an effort to seize Stuve. Now he realized that the other man stood waiting for just such a move, where the strength of those abnormal arms could be matched against the lesser arms of an opponent off balance and reaching forward.

It would be the sea-born reflexes this day that would help him more than his third-generation strength, thought Johnny. In strength, for once, he was matched.

Like chess players they watched each other for a second. Then, this time Stuve moved.

He feinted toward the pistol lying in front of the open fireplace. As Johnny flinched in that direction, the smaller man sprang suddenly around the other end of the desk.

They were facing each other now with nothing between them. Stuve was crouched over like a wrestler, legs straight, body bent from the waist and one arm outstretched, pawing in the direction of Johnny. Johnny, counting on his superior speed, dodged right suddenly, trying to trap that pawing arm in an armlock as he passed.

He was not quite quick enough. Stuve's hand closed on Johnny's forearm; they swung over together and went pinwheeling the long way of the

room. As they struck the floor at the far end, Johnny's powerful swimmer's legs kicked out toward
the body of the other man and Stuve broke loose,
dodging back to the center of the study.

Johnny was on his feet and quickly after him. In
the open space of the room before the fireplace
they began to circle each other cautiously, both
walking now in the wrestler's crouch, bent over,
right arm extended to grab.

All that had taken place so far, except for the
sound of tumbled furniture and the sound of falling bodies, had passed in silence. Stuve was not
breathing heavily. Neither did he show a flush of
effort or emotion upon his white face. He was
emotionless, calm and professional in his concentration. His eyes studied Johnny.

They had been studying each other in these
early passes between them. Now they both knew
much about each other. Both had been educated
in the deadly arts of hand-to-hand fighting and
the quick kill; Johnny at the Space Academy,
Stuve, it would be hard to tell where. Each had a
superior physical weapon. In Stuve's case it was
the strength of his strange arms. In Johnny's case
it was reflexes a shade quicker and the power of
his legs. Stuve's quick avoidance of the scissor-
hold attempt showed that the smaller man had
recognized Johnny's advantage in this. The legs
were a clumsier weapon, but for this the speed in
reflex compensated.

They were a strangely even match.

Even as Johnny noted this, Stuve moved. He
went up into the air like an attacking cat and tried
to come down on Johnny's back.

He was almost, but not quite, successful. He got

one arm around Johnny's shoulder and moving up across Johnny's throat for a choke hold, but the other arm missed its grasp. Johnny dove forward, rolling over, flinging the clinging body of the other against the edge of the desk. There was a faint, cracking sound and Stuve broke loose. But when Johnny got his feet under him and turned to face his opponent once more, Stuve held himself a little canted in his crouch, as if something was broken in his left side. They began to circle once more.

Abruptly, when his back was to the long way of the room and Johnny backed against the desk, Stuve turned and ran. The move caught Johnny unprepared and he was a shade slow in starting in pursuit. Too slow to keep Stuve from opening the door of the room and getting out into the little central hall where the escalator ramp ended.

A Johnny reached the hall, Stuve passed the ramp and dodged through the other door, into a small room that revealed itself as a solarium, full of soft air and growing plants—with another door in its far end.

To this door Stuve ran, bending sideways as if against the hurt in his side. He jerked open the door, dodged through and managed to half close it behind him against Johnny's following.

The door opened outward in Stuve's direction. Johnny, driving hard, struck it with greater weight than Stuve possessed. And all the power of his legs behind him.

But instead of opposing him, the door was jerked open before him. His thrust carried him, the door was jerked open before him. His thrust carried him forward. He had a glimpse of the sun, now flooding the sky and all the distant mountain peaks with red and brilliant light, and the rainbow-shimmering flash of the magnetic shield before him belling out beyond the balcony. —And a split-second's glimpse of a black metal railing that caught him just below the waist.

He went forward over the railing and the earth below, the lakeside with foreshortened standing shapes of men upon it whirled before his vision. Then his hands, flying backward on each side of him, closed on the same black railing that had tripped him. He swung over and down like a gymnast on the single bar, his back coming up with a jar that drove the breath from him, his palms twisting around on the railing, so that he hung with his back against the flooring of the balcony, facing outward at the air and the ground four stories below.

Instinctively, he flipped himself about, going right hand over left to grasp further along the rail and face inward before hauling himself back up over the rail onto the balcony. He looked inward to the balcony and his eyes met the eyes of Stuve, crouched and gazing at him from only a few feet away.

For once he had caught Stuve unprepared. His quickness in saving himself from the fall to his death had frozen the other for a fraction of a second of disbelief. But almost immediately Stuve was scuttling forward, and his abnormally powerful hands closed on the grasping fingers of Johnny to pry them from the railing.

A sad look clouded his eyes as he did so. It was the look of a man who does what he must—not what he desires. For a small moment he was off guard. —And in that moment Johnny pulled up his legs, reached through under the railing with them and clamped them around Stuve's waist. He pulled the smaller man out under the railing to dangle below him in mid-air above the concrete and tile flooring of the lower balcony, way below Stuve's swinging feet.

They hung. Johnny's hands held them both from a fall to the lower flooring that would cripple if not kill them. His powerful swimmer's legs were closing, closing about Stuve's waist, collasping the ribs and driving the air from Stuve's lungs.

Stuve said nothing. But before Johnny could pull them both back up onto the floor of the upper balcony, Stuve reached downward. There was an ornamental coping halfway between the upper floor and the top of the door to the lower balcony. Stuve's arms just barely stretched to catch hold of it. His long fingers closed on it and he began to pull downward against Johnny's grip on the railing.

Slowly, Johnny felt his fingers weakening against his pull and the double weight of their two bodies. Stuve hung twisted in the grasp of Johnny's legs, head downward, looking at the tile floor below. All his being seemed concentrated in pulling himself to that goal, no matter how murderous their meeting must be.

"We'll both die, this way," muttered Johnny between his locked jaws to the man below.

Stuve did not answer. He seemed determined on either escape or death. He continued to drag them both downward with all the strength of his arms.

Johnny's head swam. He had a moment of lightheadedness that brushed him like one feather of some dark wing, in which he seemed to imagine that he had hold of some unearthly, demonic force that was determined to drag him and all the world down into darkness with it. All the waters of the seas seemed to pound in his ears. A queer exhilaration filled him. The waters buoyed him up. He felt that he would never let go. His legs tightened.

And just then Stuve's hands dragged his hands loose from the railing.

There was a flashing moment in mid-air. Stuve tried to turn like a cat and free himself, but was only partially successful. He was a little underneath when the impact came. A heavy blow blotted out the light from Johnny's eyes. The light came back. Johnny's head jarred with a cruel sickening pain. Then, slowly, the jarring diminished and he raised his head.

He was lying a few feet away from Stuve. He remembered then that he had not held on until the actual moment of impact after all. Instinct had loosened his legs from the other man's waist in the instant of falling. He had kicked free and that kicking free had possibly saved his life.

Stuve lay almost on his back, crumpled on the tile. His head was bleeding and there was a little blood on his mouth. His eyelids fluttered and he looked at Johnny. He, too, was still alive—but barely.

Distantly, Johnny heard the whiplike double crack of twin energy arcs blowing a magnetic field, and the shield around the tower disap-

peared as a soap bubble pops. He heard feet rushing up the outside staircase to the balcony.

He paid them no attention. He pulled himself
upright into a sitting position and his head swam.
He bent over Stuve, who looked up into his face.

"Now," whispered Stuve with great effort
through his bloody mouth, ". . . your way. But
you'll see . . ."

The running feet were almost to the balcony.
Johnny ignored them. Stuve was trying to say
something more.

". . . I leave you . . . the . . . world . . ." His
whisper faltered and failed. "For your . . ." He
could get no more words out. His eyes clouded a
little and it seemed his gaze wandered. Then he
choked, suddenly, coughed up blood, and died.

Johnny sat staring at the dead man with his
head pounding and ringing. The feel of a hand on
his shoulder woke him and he looked up to see the
face of Pat, looking down.

"Pat . . ." he said, dully. "So you're all right."

"I'm all right," said the lean face of Pat. "How
about you?"

"All right . . . I think . . ." Johnny made an
effort to rise. Pat helped him. He got to his feet and
swayed there, looking around him. At the foot of
the tower were the sea-born with other armed men
and the black, suitcase-like shapes of the arc
equipment that had blown the magnetic shield of
the tower. A movement in the sky where the sunset was fading, and the sun was down, caught his
eye. It was a black flying shape, coming in fast
from the east for a landing by the tower. He
blinked and looked again, and recognized it. It

was one of the ships captured from the Hunters in their raid on the sea-lab.

"Help me down," he said to Pat. And with Pat balancing he stumbled down the outside steps to the ground, just as the Hunter ship settled to the ground amongst the wreckage there. Its door opened. Maytig jumped out and ran to him.

"Johnny!" she said. "You're hurt?"

"I'm all right," he said. "What're you here for?"

"It's Kai Ebberly," she answered, staring at him. Her blue eyes were hard as chips of sapphire. "As soon as he heard you'd gotten in here—"

"He's gone back on his bargain with us?"

She stared at him, nodding.

"You said his word was no good," she answered. She shivered, abruptly and uncontrollably. "What can we do now?"

He forced the pounding ache clear from his brain for a second.

"You're going to take me back to the spaceship," he said. "Pat—" He turned to his cousin. "You get Mila Jhan and get back to the Barons. Do what you can to make them hold off any action until they've talked to the Sea Captains. Maytig will get the Captains and bring them to a meeting ashore—say, in the Terminal Building at Savannah Stand."

"And you?" Pat demanded. "What are you going to do now?"

"I?" Johnny became suddenly conscious that the pain in his head had been causing him to clench the muscles of his jaw against it, until those muscles, too, ached. With an effort he forced them to relax and heard himself speak less tightly.

"Tomi and I are heading back into space—for one last try at the Space Swimmers."

For a second Pat and Maytig stood without answering, staring at him.

"You think," said Pat at last, "that the Swimmers can be any hope to us *now*?"

"Now and ever," replied Johnny. "Right from the very beginning, whether we knew it or not, they've been the only hope we had."

# 16

Pat took Maytig's ship to return to the Ebberly Estates. Johnny, Maytig herself, and the rest of the sea-born headed away in one of the transport ships that had brought them to Stuve's mountain top, back toward the waters of the North Atlantic. They ended this return trip in forty fathoms of water beside the Atlantic Headquarters Home—and the dark, enormous length of the spaceship that still hung there, underwater, waiting.

Not merely moments but several hours after that were required to get the spaceship back out to the halfway mark between the orbits of Earth and Mars. But, at last, they reached their destination point.

"I wish I had your confidence," Leif said, as he watched Johnny and Tomi strap on their five-hour oxygen packs. "What makes you think you can pass over like Tomi does?"

"I just think it," said Johnny. "That's all I can tell you. If I could explain to you why I thought so, we'd probably already have the Swimmers' secret."

"And even if you do pass over," said Leif. "What makes you think you can get a Space Swimmer to tell you something none of them could or would tell Tomi?"

"We'll be going after an older one. The oldest we can find."

"The older ones won't speak to Tomi."

"I think they'll speak to me."

"Why?" demanded Leif, almost exasperated.

"Because"—Johnny's eyes moved to his son for a second—"I'm an adult."

Leif opened his mouth, then closed it and shook his head. He walked around behind Johnny.

"Let me help you with that oxygen pack," he said.

Fifteen minutes later, Tomi and Johnny emerged together from the spaceship and pushed away from it on their ion-drives with their backs to the dwindled but brilliant orb of the sun.

Ahead of them the stars hung in their countless numbers. After only a little distance Tomi shut off his ion-drive and Johnny followed his son's example. He saw Tomi apparently hanging still in space and he tried to reach out and feel one of the invisible roads of the Swimmers, as he had the time before.

Much more quickly than it had happened before he began to be aware of the singing, golden current running about him. He looked and saw the magnetic envelope, faintly on each side of him, rippling as if to unseen pressures. The singing sensation mounted in him. The feeling of identification and response that came with following the strange paths. Now the space road along which he traveled sang through Johnny's whole mind and body, bringing him a heightened awareness, a brightness of perception he had never felt so fully before.

The multi-colored jewels of the stars about him had never shone with such brightness. The empty vacuum of space itself seemed to be charged, alive with thought and texture. He felt it about and upon and enclosing the magnetic envelope that enclosed him, like a piece of cloth, enclosed and wavering in an offshore tide, being carried out to sea.

Just so had he watched the gossamer gas bodies of the swimmers rippling from false-windows, the vision screens of the training spaceship in his Academy days.

"Dad!" It was Tomi's voice over the radio circuit between them. "Look! Look there, up ahead!"

Johnny looked. It took him a moment to find it, but then he saw it, still small with distance, the ice-blue form of a Space Swimmer. He strained mentally and emotionally to see if he could get any feeling of its presence through the force road itself. And he seemed to feel something. . . . It was only an impression, but he got a sensation of something massive and majestic and remote.

"He's not young?" Johnny asked.

"He's old!" came back Tomi's voice. "He's so old. . . . I can't tell you how old. Older than anyone, I think, Dad." Tomi's voice became charged with excitement, suddenly. "Look at him try to get away. I told you."

The Swimmer changed direction up ahead suddenly. And, for the first time, Johnny seemed to glimpse a pattern of the forces before him through which an interconnection could be traced from Tomi and himself to the Swimmer. It was like seeing without seeing. Without conscious effort, he followed Tomi, swinging over onto a road—he saw them again, now like girders of golden light stretching through the darkness—on the trail of the ancient Swimmer. He found himself right behind his son. And he, Tomi, and the Swimmer were all accelerating.

"Look out!" sang Tomi. "We're going to pass over!"

Johnny braced himself against being left behind. But just then, inconceivably but actually before him, he saw it. One of the portal points beyond which was a portion of ordinary space and time far distant from the solar system. His new perceptions of the magnetic forces perceived it, like a hoop of blazing fire through the center of which ran the road he was now on. Even as he saw it, he was at it. There was a sudden, soft flare of force about him, and a feeling that was not, but felt like, a slight, abrupt change in pressure of his body.

He blinked and saw Tomi and the Space Swimmer just before him. The enormous, dull red orb of a strange sun burned like some great, sullen ruby to their right. And all of the surrounding stars were different.

Johnny's feeling of exultation at passing over was lost in the continuing anxiety of the chase.

The three of them fled together through the different space. In the carmine wash of light from the other star the Swimmer was an undulating expanse of violet color; and Tomi, just ahead of his father, seemed dipped in crimson. In this new light of a different burning sun, for a moment Johnny felt himself blinded to the space roads. Then they emerged, as objects emerge to the vision of eyes blinded by the brighter light of a different room. He saw them, glowing like a maze of golden girders again, on all sides of him.

The Swimmer drove on without slackening its flight. Three more times it changed roads and then, abruptly, passed over once more, bursting through into yet another part of space. This time a white-hot pinpoint of light hung off to their left and on their right there flashed by without warning a huge and lifeless chunk of rock like a mountain torn up by the roots and thrown away. Seemingly they passed within a few miles of it.

Then the Swimmer passed over again. They were all lost in an endless garden of star-jewelled void, the suns more thickly clustered than those to be seen in the night sky of Earth.

"He won't stop. He just won't talk!" said Tomi's voice, grimly, in the receiver of Johnny's mask.

They passed over again, into the light of a sun yellower and larger than the sun of Earth, and with a blazingly bright star not far from it in that quadrant of space surrounding them. A feeling came to Johnny that they were far from home.

"Do you know how to get back, Tomi?" Johnny asked over the radio circuit.

"Uh-huh. Sure . . ."

Tomi's voice was weary-sounding and dulled.

Jarred out of his intoxication with the roads, the chase, and all the colors of the stars, Johnny glanced at the chronometer on his wrist. He stared at it, hardly able to believe what he saw. Over two hours had passed already since they had left the spaceship. For the first time, he was conscious himself of weariness, like the kind of nervous exhaustion that comes from high and joyous excitement prolonged over a period of hours.

He recognized that he felt somehow drained— as if this apparently effortless flight was using up some vital store of strength within him.

"How do you get back?" he asked Tomi, sharply.

"Well . . . it's sort of down and over—you know!" the boy's voice, as well as being tired, was vague. "You just keep going in the right direction until you feel it. Then you know where it is, and you go there. . . ."

"How do you know where it is?" The boy did not answer. "Tomi!"

"You feel it . . . You know, like this . . . Dad," said Tomi, "I'm getting worn out. With the younger ones we don't keep going steady like this. . . ."

"Hang on," said Johnny. "We've got to keep after him. I've got to stay with him until he stops, and then I've got to make him talk. Maybe it won't be much longer we'll have to chase him. He ought to be getting tired, too."

"Maybe . . ." sighed Tomi, heavily. "He's old . . . and stronger than . . .

The boy's voice trailed off without finishing its sentence. They went on. Without warning, the

Swimmer passed over three times quickly, so that they flickered in and out of different solar systems. Johnny saw them, one after the other, like frames of a film strip jamming in an old fashioned movie projector he had seen run once in a museum ashore. When they came out into the third and final space, Johnny saw that he was now closest to the Swimmer. Tomi was lagging behind them both.

"Keep up, Tomi!" Johnny called over the radio circuit.

"I can't . . ." the voice of the boy was throaty with weariness. And feeling the exhaustion rising inside himself, Johnny could not blame his son. "I just. . . . can't. . . ."

The Swimmer passed over once more. Johnny followed, and looked back.

Tomi was no longer with them.

Johnny had no time to think of it. Immediately the Swimmer was passing over again, and changing roads. Tomi, Johnny remembered, had said he knew his way back to the spaceship. Johnny settled his mind with that thought and clung to the trail of the Swimmer with undivided mind. Now the great space creature was passing over again and again, as if in a desperate, final series of attempts to shake off its single remaining pursuer.

Worlds and suns flickered for a moment before Johnny's eyes before they were replaced by the worlds and suns of other systems. Desert planets whose disk was a solid shade of uniform grayish white. Huge planets wreathed in atmospheres of colorful gases. Green-blue planets of land and sea like the Earth; and all-blue planets showing only a dot of land here or there in a world-wide ocean that woke all the sea-instinct in Johnny and something more.

With its awakening he began gradually to examine and bring into focus the sensations that were reaching through his magnetic envelope to him. His mind, trained by six years of introspection and self-examination, began to sort and classify and relate the data it was receiving through his various senses. Slowly he began to make sense of this environment of the space roads.

When the Swimmer had first begun to fling his great blue form through pass-over point after pass-over point in rapid succession, Johnny had automatically turned on his ion-drive during a moment of ordinary space, and pulled up almost within touching distance of the wavering gaseous body. Now they fled close together through the interstellar distances. And from this closeness and his growing experience with the sensation of space-road travel, Johnny began to explore—now that the first amazement and shock had worn off.

His own weariness he had held at bay by emotion and will, so far. Now it occurred to him that the Swimmer was deliberately forcing him to use up whatever particular faculty of the living organism was drained by the effort of space-road travel. The moment he thought this, he was aware of the fact that the Swimmer was less tired than he was. He examined this new knowledge.

In the sensation coming from the giant he pursued was the concept of massiveness; but also a thread of fear on the part of the Swimmer. A thread that connected to a potential of equal massiveness in Johnny's self.

For some reason, the Swimmer was afraid. Therefore he could not simply assume that he would run Johnny between the stars until Johnny dropped, as Tomi had, from exhaustion. Therefore there was more to his actions than straightforward flight.

Aroused, Johnny began to study the pattern of the spaceroads about him and the route the blue Space Swimmer was tracing through their maze. His mind, disciplined by the six years of struggling to understand the causative pattern ashore, examined and studied the pattern of the spaceroads.

Slowly, the balance and purpose of their pattern emerged.

As the ear untrained to interpreting a foreign language hears only a continuous babble of noise at first, so his mind had seen only an incomprehensible galaxy-wide and galaxy-deep confusion in the space-roads. But Leif had said that there must be more to them than that. That, like the pattern of interconnecting forces of the magnetic fields of the magnetic envelopes and irises, they must be in balance. Their joinings and divergences could not be chance, but must represent a continual attempt to balance the forces flowing along the roads. Just as the causal pattern attempted continually to restore the sociological balance disturbed by individual actions. Slowly, he began to perceive these shapes of balance in the space-roads.

They existed, he saw, as a structure of girders might exist inside a globe to support the outer skin of the globe—where that outer skin was the ordinary space-time facet of the galaxy. Near the galactic center the roads were thickly clustered, thinning out toward the galaxy's edge. But locally, even as small interconnecting struts or spars between the larger space-road girders, the roads did not fill all space uniformly.

With the roads, too, every advantage implied a limitation. Where there were none of the girders, struts, or spars of magnetic lines in space, the Space Swimmers could not go. The more important the girder, the more swiftly a Swimmer travelled it, and the longer it went without an intersection, the further the distance of ordinary space–time that was covered in the moment of passing over when the point of intersection came.

To Johnny, suddenly, it was something like the antarctic waters, around the berg-Home, and the pack ice. In the free corridors of water, in, around, and below the ice chunks sea-swimmers could travel. As he and the Swimmer now travelled in, around, above, and below the roadless areas of space. The Swimmer fled before Johnny, and Johnny chased it like some hunted quarry, but the Swimmer was choosing the route to his own advantage.

He—or it—was taking advantage of a greater knowledge of the pattern of the space-roads to make Johnny's effort of following greater than the effort of fleeing. In physical terms it was hard to describe, but the Swimmer consistently passed over at a more convenient moment than did Johnny behind him, and the great blue shape turned off from one road to another consistently at a slightly easier angle than the man who must follow behind.

Johnny was, he saw, being maneuvered into

exhausting himself, as one chess player might maneuver another into a position where defeat was inevitable.

Johnny turned to an examination of the space-road pattern itself. It was like the causative pattern. It built outward from the principle of the existence of the galaxy, as the causative pattern built outward from the principle of the existence of the human mind—which *thought*, therefore it *was*.

Now that he looked along the pattern, he saw the enormous stretches of the roads, running from star to farther star, from spiral arm across fifty thousand light-years to the galactic center. The roads built outward from that galactic center like a growth of crystals, of which the roads were the internal, shape-sustaining forces. As their overall pattern became apparent to him, a sense of orientation developed in Johnny. Toward the galactic center was down. All directions outward from that, but particularly toward the tips of the spiral arms, were up.

A sudden sense of giddiness flowed through him. Like a man leaning out the open door of a helicopter, who gazes at the ground six hundred feet below, and is not bothered—then watches a cable descend, down and down, until at last it's all but invisible and hovers above earth far below. Before, for the man in the helicopter, the ground might have been a model image, only a few feet down. Now his eyes measure the actual descending length of the line and each foot of empty space is counted by the sudden vertigo of his senses. So Johnny's mind suddenly, for the first time, measured the great, swooping, plummeting distances

and depths of the galaxy along the glowing, golden paths of the lines of magnetic force that were the space-roads.

He felt like an insect unexpectedly discovering himself high on the metal skeleton of some titanic building greater than man had ever built or dreamed of building.

He conquered the giddiness. It was a luxury he could not afford now. He had seen the pattern of the roads, and it was up to him to match the Space Swimmer in their use. Slowly he allowed the pattern of the space-roads to build, as the original analog had built in that introspective universe of his mind in the berg-Home. Holding a new analog, one of the space-road pattern, in his mind's eye, he began to work with it.

Now for the first time, he did not follow the great blue Swimmer. He began to herd the other.

The Swimmer fled. It was more than ordinary desire to avoid contact that lent drive to its flight. It was a demand, a duty, a complete dedication to the thought of escape. And because escape, to it, was more important than anything else, it came about that Johnny was at last able to direct the general shape of their movement.

He was driving the Space Swimmer outward from the center, upward toward the galaxy's edge, and the spiral arms. What had been a thick interlocking of roads was now becoming an open lattice, more open with each succeeding passing-over.

—Now the lattice had become a ladder, a few interconnections between two main roads towering up into darkness.

Now suddenly there were two roads no longer.

There was one only, like a great shaft reaching past only occasional intersections up and out into intergalactic darkness.

Their pace had increased beyond comprehension. Now they broke, frequently, passing over in direct line of flight because they could not be contained in ordinary space-time. In Johnny, something like a fury mounted.

He had not let go of Stuve before Stuve dragged him from the railing. That much he had done to achieve the end he fought for. He would not let go now of this old man of the void racing before him. Now, with each flickering change, the stars were growing thinnner in all quarters. As if up a pole as long as eternity they fled together. Great gaps and rents of darkness grew about them. Wider and wider grew the darkness. Less and less the stars.

Now, directly ahead of them the blackness was broken only by two or three hazy, distant illuminations, like street lamps seen from far off through a foggy and lightless distance. Looking back Johnny saw the stars behind them gathered together and shrunk to an ellipsoidal shape, like a jewelled eye in the darkness.

Distantly from that far eye their single road projected on upward into nothingness. Distantly the foggy little lamps in the blackness hung unchanging. And with a cold, brilliant sense of realization, Johnny recognized that they were the lights of other galaxies, other island universes shrunk by their millions of light-years of distance. In the dark Johnny could no longer see the wide, undulating surface of the blue Swimmer, but he could feel the other's presence also upon the road, and he spoke out loud.

"Go ahead," he said. "Wherever you go. I'll go with you."

With that, taking him unawares for he had never expected that the Swimmer would hear and understand him, he felt a voiceless sudden cry in answer. It was an emission of pure emotion, like the sound of a guitar string snapping in exhaustion and tension beyond bearing. Unexpectedly the vast invisible shape ceased its headlong flight, ceased its undulations. It let the original impetus of its movement take it away like a drowning creature in an offshore tide.

Johnny gave up as well. In the same moment, he abandoned the effort of his chase and the two of them floated outwards from the galaxy of their birth like two sea-born fighters under the waves, locked and dying together.

They drifted, washed by the same exhaustion, drowning in the same cessation of effort. The magnetic current of the space-road bound them together, and unhindered perceptions leaked back and forth between them. Johnny felt the alien presence as close as that of another human breathing exhausted beside him in the dark. An abrupt, unsuspected sympathy for the great Space creature washed through him—and suddenly—the patterns slid together, and matched.

The darkness that surrounded them, the barrier between them, seemed to split apart for one fractional moment of realization; and to Johnny came, sharply and clearly, the wild outburst of astonishment on the part of the Space Swimmer. It was astonishment like that a man might have felt on hearing a parrot stop jabbering and abruptly enunciate Newton's law of cooling in connection

with a sunflower seed dropped into the drinking
bowl of its cage. On the backwash of that astonishment came a flood of questioning from the
Swimmer, expressed in terms of the magnetic
flow of forces and of the experience which man
and Swimmer shared.

To Johnny it was like being in the midst of an
explosion of fireworks, enwrapped in subtle
tastes, drowning in a flood of music through
which came the chant of some mighty poem of
purpose. It swelled about him, leaving him without understanding. But he had expected that.

"Yes, I'm mature," he said. "I think that's what
you're asking. We mature more more swiftly than
you do. The other smaller being was my son—but
you don't understand that do you? It means he's
not mature yet, just as you felt he wasn't."

Once more came the flood of questioning. It was
impossible to tell whether the Space Swimmer
had understood or not. But Johnny had planned
for this moment.

Within his magnetic envelope, in the interstellar dark, he began to pantomime, with swimming
motions, as if he danced.

# 17

Birds, animals, and fish migrate, finding their way often through unfamiliar or chartless territory, often to a destination that their generation has never seen before. The effect of currents in the oceans, seasonal changes in temperature, length of day and sunlight offered partial solutions to how this could be accomplished. But only with the charting of the deep magnetic movements in the Earth's core, with their relation to the orientation sense among the third generation of the sea-People, was the common lodestar of all migrations uncovered.

The linear magnetic and supra-magnetic forces were ubiquitous. They existed everywhere. In the living cell, as in the bodies of certain types of marching termites who had been observed much earlier to line themselves up with the Earth's

magnetic field. In the paramagnetism of most
chemical elements and many compounds. In the
minute electrical discharges of living brain and
muscles. They existed, they could be sensed, they
could be not only traveled as in the case of the
space-roads—but interpreted—and read.

Ants read them to coordinate the activities of
the ant hill. Bees read them in the movements of
the worker bee, returned to the hive, who
"danced" to announce where and how far from
the hive she had found a source of nectar. The
female bower bird read them in the dance of the
courting male. And animal-men, without a real
language back in the early shadows of prehistory,
had read them in the movements of other
animal-men dancing the story of a successful
hunt from which they had just returned.

The big blue Space Swimmer read them in the
rhythmic disturbance of the magnetic forces
caused by Johnny's dance. It was a crude and
primitive means of communication on Johnny's
part, but any other would have failed. The conditions of life upon the surface of one of the solid
bodies in space was as unimaginable to the
Swimmer as life on the endless invisible network
of the space-roads would have been to Earth-
bound man before he had lifted his eyes to look
out from his small world into space. But both
conditions could be expressed in the magnetic
flows and variances. Johnny danced extem-
poraneously, as the animal-men had danced, letting his mental images dictate the movements of
his body, each movement of which broadcast its
coded patterns of the linear forces.

Meanwhile, they two were falling back toward the body of the galaxy. When they had ceased their outward driving they had fallen off the road they had been following outward, and onto the first weak, returning crossroad that intersected it. The mass of the galaxy, expressed in a control concentration of its magnetic forces drew them back toward its center. They fell back at any angle, until they intersected a stronger road, also returning toward the mass of the galactic center. And took that.

And, with his last remaining oxygen, Johnny strove to pantomine the story of the history of the human race, ending in the four generations of the sea-People and the conflict between Land and Sea. But when he pantomined his desire to question the Space Swimmer on the single subject that had brought him along the long, hard, way to this moment—communication failed. He could feel the other no longer understood.

The Space Swimmer returned a flood of questions of his own. But as before, Johnny was helpless to understand in his turn.

Something more was needed. If Tomi had only been able to keep up with him on the long chase . . . Johnny took a shallow breath. His pack of frozen oxygen was failing at last and the breath brought him little energy. Once more he tried to express physically the message that the Swimmer should seek out other humans like his son, and try to talk to them. But his strength was failing. His limbs fumbled. His lungs strained for the material of life that was not available and darkness began to creep in on the edges of his vision . . .

A distant shout jarred him from the slumber that was now attracting him like some weary traveler to a downy bed.

" . . . Dad! *Dad!*" It was the voice of Tomi, shouting over the radio circuit. "Hold still, Dad! Hold still, so I can put this fresh oxygen pack on, and get it connected for you!"

Defeated, the darkness drew back. He breathed deeply and looked around him. He was sliding along a force-road in the light of a near-orange sun, and with him was the great blue rippling shape of the Swimmer, and Tomi.

"Where . . ." Johnny blinked at the boy. "Where did you come from?"

"I just went back to the ship. I got tired, you know," said Tomi. "Leif gave me something to eat and drink and a red pill to take. Then I felt better. I got a fresh oxygen pack myself, and got one for you, and came back."

"But—" Johnny stared at him. "How did you find me?"

Tomi stared back.

"But, you know!" he said, at last. "It's just like in the sea, Dad. You just go where people ought to be!"

Johnny blinked. The connection between the orientation of the sea-creatures and the sea-born in the oceans, and the orientation of the Swimmers in space, being both in origin responsive to surrounding magnetic forces, had slipped his mind under the pressure of other matters. Now that he thought of it, it was quite reasonable that sea and space creatures should both orient themselves magnetically. An individual, being part of the pattern, could be "felt" and therefore located as well as any other pattern element. —Though, for Johnny, in space, that ability would have to be learned the hard way.

Tomi possessed it instinctively and naturally, apparently, as part of his fourth-generation senses. But he was undoubtedly the only living human who did. Only by use of an analog pattern would Johnny be able to find his way on the roads. That was why Tomi was so important—and the risk of him, that was coming, would be so great.

But there was no time to think about the future now. Back on Earth the talks between the Sea Captains and Ebberly, which Johnny had suggested to gain Tomi and himself time in space, would be wearing thin. He must communicate with this Swimmer now, or never.

"Tomi," he said. "I can feel this Space Swimmer talking to me, but I can't understand him and he can't understand me. Can you interpret for us?"

"Sure?" Tomi stared at his father curiously. "You can't understand him at all? He's asking all sorts of questions. He says—"

"Hold it," interrupted Johnny. "I don't suppose time means anything to him, but it does to us. We've got only a little time before we have to get back to the ship. Tell him that I'll answer his questions at another time—"

"He'll tell you some other time, Blue Counselor," said Tomi, turning his head to speak toward the Swimmer. "Right now we haven't much time." He turned back to Johnny, waiting.

"Blue Counselor?" said Johnny.

"That's what he calls himself," answered Tomi. "It's because he's old, and wise—"

"Never mind that now," said Johnny. "I want you to tell him what I tell you, and ask him just to tell me whether what I say is right. Just that."

"—My dad's going to tell you something," Tomi said to the great, blue form beside them. "You answer yes or no."

He looked back at Johnny, waiting.

"There's a necessary understanding," said Johnny slowly, "needed at a certain point of growth in the life of an individual—" He paused to let Tomi repeat his words to the Swimmer. "An understanding of an evolutionary ethic—"

"What's 'ethic' ?" asked Tomi, checking short at the word.

"A system of rules, moral rules, for growing and developing."

"—Things you have to know and do to grow right, Blue Counselor," translated Tomi. "Go on, Dad. Blue Counselor says 'Yes,' by the way."

"This ethic," said Johnny, "involves—has to have, Tomi—three concepts. —Three ideas. These ideas have to be achieved, or known, before the first stage of evolution is finished and the second stage begun."

He paused and nodded at Tomi.

"These things you have to know," said Tomi to the Space Swimmer, "they've got three parts. And you have to have all the parts to go up a notch in growing up."

"The concepts," said Johnny, "are the concepts of *freedom, responsibility,* and *work*—and particularly *work.*"

Tomi translated.

For a moment after he had translated, he hung

silent. Then, slowly he shook his head and turned to Johnny.

"He says—" the boy hesitated. "I can tell you, Dad, but it doesn't make much sense."

"Tell me anyway," said Johnny.

"He says—" Tomi fumbled for words. "It was dark to begin with, falling into the light of the roads. And a long falling, and then a new light that was inside but further than any star. And a great fear and sorrow for time past, but then a changing and afterwards no more falling. But a long climb to the new light, beyond which there is no seeing until you pass over through it—and are gone." He ran down and stared at his father. "I don't understand."

"I do," said Johnny. "Tell him I'll see him in times to come. Now—let's go. If you can find it for me, we've got something important to pick up on our way back to the space ship and Earth."

# 18

"—Maytig?" said Johnny into the spaceship transmitter.

The returning ship was falling swiftly toward the ocean surface of Savannah Stand.

"Here," the answer came back in the clicks of the dolphin code from the small transceiver Maytig or one of the Sea Captains would be wearing. "It's all right. We're still talking with the Land."

"Where are you?"

"In the Terminal Building, upstairs in one of the Conference Rooms. The Terminal's been cleared. Are you on your way, Johnny?"

"Be there in fifteen minutes. I'll sign off now." Johnny clicked off the transmitter and straightened up to look into the false-window, the vision screen showing the surface of the Earth below, toward which they were dropping.

It had been fourteen hours since they had lifted from the sea. They were coming back down into the ocean just off Savannah Stand. Looking down on the Stand and the Terminal from the air now, Johnny could see two arcs of lights almost meeting in a circle. One was an arc of searchlights twelve miles long and curving through Savannah Complex around the area of the Stand, which must signalize the grouping of Land troops and military equipment in a cordon sealing off that section of the shore. The other arc was of lights more scattered, but patterned, some fathoms below the Sea's surface and curving around to cover the same stretch of shore from the Sea. They were the lights of the smallboats and small-Homes of the fighting forces of the sea.

The arcs opposed each other, making two halves of a burning circle of light, which the sea-edge of Savannah Stand cut in two. Just inside that edge, in the darkness and stillness of the Stand, was the single, lighted shape of the Terminal Building.

The spaceship came down into the sea about eight hundred yards offshore. In a smallboat Johnny and Tomi drove in to the Stand and mounted the outside steps from the sea and went through the entrance, taking the escalator ramps to the Conference Room on the top floor. Those already there did not notice their arrival. Ebberly, his Barons, the Sea Captains, and Maytig were all at the end of the long room running between the corridor by which Johhny and Tomi had just entered, and the wall-length window set in the side of the Terminal on this floor. The framed outer blackness of this window reflected the overhead lighting in the room, like a slab of polished obsidian. Between the harsh, floating lights above, the gleaming floor, the blank wall hiding the corridor, and the polished lightlessness of the long window, the room was like the arena for some surgical amputation in a duel with death.

"Tomi," said Johnny quietly, stopping just outside the entrance. "I want you to watch Ebberly for me. Warn me when you think it's necessary. You'll do that?"

Tomi's eyes looked gravely back up at him, seeming to shimmer slightly at this close range, because Johnny himself had put on not one of the single magnetic, sea-pressure envelopes, but one of the double magnetic envelopes they had used in space.

"I'll tell you," said Tomi. They went on in.

The tensions in the room were like wires strung tautly across his path. Johnny could almost feel them against his skin as he walked forward. At the far end of the room Ebberly and the other Barons—including Mila Jhan on the end—were seated behind a long table. Pat stood not with the sea-People, but behind Mila. Facing these were the Sea Captains, with Maytig amongst them. She had on the short-skirted dress that the women of the sea-People had used to wear for visits ashore. But the Sea Captains wore trunks, magnetic envelopes, and weapon belts clipped with shark knives and side arms.

Under the hard and glittering overhead lights, they seemed to loom above the fragile slimness of Mila, and the squat, middle-aged forms of the seated Barons. The lithe, powerful, and clean-limbed bodies of the People made squat and sub-human by contrast the men of the shore. Alone, among the seated men, Kai Ebberly's square, brutal face under its brindle hair, in the center of the group, seemed still to blaze with an innate, primitive strength. Beside him, Wally Kutch looked fatter and older than ever.

". . . We're talking in circles," Ebberly was saying harshly as Johnny and Tomi came in. "You won't back up this threat of yours with any facts. You know about the *salmonella* mutant. There's no secret about it. It's a laboratory mutation of the bacteria that causes one type of food poisoning. An independent, free-swimming form. If we turn it loose in the oceans it'll infect everything—fish, plankton, seaweed, everything like that, that can carry it and live. But you and the warm blooded sea-mammals will eat it—and die. Now," he grin-ned ferociously across the table. "That's fact. That's plain speaking. But what've you got to match it?"

"We told you," said Maytig.

"That you can sink the land." Ebberly's voice was as heavy and cruel as a meat cleaver coming down on a chopping block. "I don't believe it. Anyone can say something like that. You know that bacteria can be subjected to controlled mutations—but I don't know that continents can be sunk. Why should I believe you?"

"Because," said Johnny, pushing through the Sea Captains with Tomi following until the two of them stood facing Ebberly only about a dozen feet from the desk, "they've been sunk before."

"Oh, there you are!" said Ebberly, sitting back

in his chair and grinning harshly. "I've been waiting for you. Now maybe we can get down to business. I want your people ashore and wearing my
Mark inside of eighty-six hours. That's the offer I
made you in the first place—"

"No," said Johnny.

"Look—" said Ebberly, drawing out the word
long and hard. He leaned forward on his elbows
on the table and picked up two pens that were
laying there, holding each in his fist like a miniature club. "You can't stay in the sea. We're going
to make the sea uninhabitable."

"You'll be dead yourself first," said Johnny,
evenly. "You didn't seem to hear me, just now. I
told you the continents had been drowned before."

"Oh?" said Ebberly, grinning at him. "By
whom?"

"Nature," said Johnny. "Did you ever hear of
the Ring of Fire?"

"No," said Ebberly. He threw himself back in
his chair but held onto the two pens. "Never heard
of it."

"It's in the geology books," said Johnny. "A line
of volcanic activity in and beside the continents
bordering on the deep basin of the Pacific Ocean.
It rings the basin, covering a third of the globe.
There're other chains of volcanic activity like it
elsewhere in the world. They represent the bor-
derlines, the frontiers between the conflicting
crustal forces of submergence and emergence in
their present state of balance."

"Balance?" said Ebberly.

"Did you ever hear of the Tethys Sea?"

"No," said Ebberly. "Not that either." He laid the pens' tips together on the table before him.

"It existed," said Johnny, "fifty to thirty million years ago. It's in the geology books, too. There're artists' conceptions of what it looked like."

"Not my line," said Ebberly watching the pens as he nudged them into different angles with each other.

"It was an intrusion of the sea into Europe and Asia during the Eocene epoch of geological history," said Johnny. "The Tethys Sea was the Mediterranean gone wild. It covered land in southern Europe, northern Africa, and Asia Minor. It stretched on even into India and Burma. In the same geological epoch, here in North America there were drownings of the Atlantic and Pacific Coast, and the Gulf of Mexico flooded northward into southern Illinois." He turned to look at Maytig. "The geologists on the land know about this, don't they?"

She nodded. Her face was pale, as was Mila's on the other side of the table, but calm.

"They've known for nearly two hundred years," she said. "The sands and marls of the Tethys Sea are there to be seen where you said its waters went. The sediments marking their borders are called the Flysch. The Land knows. In Colorado and Wyoming, there are other depositions from the sea that covered the area during the Eocene Period."

Johnny turned back to look at Ebberly.

"That's it," he said. "Basing their work on the work of John Joly, a twentieth-century geologist, our people found where to bore into the sea-bottom, to the level of the Mororovicic Discontinuity, and set nuclear charges. If we blow them, we can trigger off a widespread submergence of the present continents.

He stopped. Ebberly, not watching him, was still playing with the pens.

"You understand?" said Johnny. "The flooding, the earthquakes and the rest of it would destroy your cities and probably most of your population. In the sea we'd keep to deep water, far from land. There'd be tidal waves and submarine earthquakes, but they'd do no damage to us. Afterwards, the deep sea would be mostly the same, but nearly all the land left would be drowned sea-bottom raised up. It'd be a thousand years before it could be all green and as it was again. And once the charges are fired, the crustal changes couldn't be halted."

Ebberly looked up from his pens and squinted at Johnny.

"Move a little closer," he said. "I can't see you so well . . ."

In fact, it seemed to have grown subtly darker in the room, though the window was still black with outer darkness and the lights still blazed overhead.

The floor was a pattern of foot-square black and white tiles. Johnny had been standing on a black tile. He moved forward half a step to stand on a white one.

"You don't believe it," he said to Ebberly.

"No," said Ebberly, looking back down at the pens.

"Because," said Johnny. "it doesn't make any difference to you whether it's true or not."

Ebberly's fingers stilled on the pens. He looked up at Johnny. His eyes were hooded by his drooping, swollen-looking eyelids.

"That's a strange thing to say," he said, with unusual quietness.

"But it's true, isn't it?" said Johnny. "If you don't get the sea-People ashore the way you want them, it doesn't matter what happens to the land as far as you're concerned."

Ebberly grinned suddenly and savagely at him.

"Go on," he said.

"I am," answered Johnny. He glanced up and down the table. For a moment his eyes met the eyes of Pat, standing behind Mila Jhan, and there was a question in Pat's eyes. Johnny shook his head almost imperceptibly, and looked back at Ebberly. "You're a great player of The Game of Life, Ebberly. Stuve was a massive talent—one of the great minds that come along in the human race about every five hundred years. But he underestimated you."

"So did you," said Ebberly.

"No," said Johnny. "I knew you planned to use me to get rid of Stuve for you. I knew from the first you wouldn't keep the agreement you made to leave the sea-People alone when I went to get Stuve at the hunting lodge."

"Why'd you go then?" said Ebberly, apparently undisturbed.

"I knew that Stuve had to be taken out of the situation," said Johnny. "And I wanted you to demonstrate something publicly—that your word, the word you talked about so constantly, really meant nothing to you."

"It meant something," said Ebberly.

"But not enough," answered Johnny. "Not compared to what you were really after. I said Stuve was a great talent. How great the world's going to find out in the coming years. But he was like a stage magician among gorillas. He underestimated them. He took you at face value."

"Why not?" asked Ebberly, picking up the pens once more.

"Because that was the biggest trap about you," Johnny said. "You painted yourself as a man who had wealth and power—the most of everything. You'd won The Game. You were King of the Castle, top man in the world. So, you said, you didn't have any need to be anything but altruistic. You were too big for ambition you said—only, you weren't."

Ebberly played with the pens, watching them. He did not answer.

"You weren't content with top place in this world, and time," said Johnny. "You wanted the top place in History—to be the man who sent the human race out to the far stars. And for that you were sure you needed the sea-People working for you to find the way. And you didn't care what it cost, so you got us."

"And I've done that," said Ebberly, not looking up from the pens. "I'm willing to use the *salmonella* mutation. And whether you've got this Ring of Fire thing of yours or not doesn't matter, you know, because you wouldn't have the guts to use it and kill three billion people." He looked up then at Johnny, harshly grinning. "You see, I understand you people, and I'm going to be the man who unlocks the space-road after all."

"No," answered Johnny. "Not any more. That road's already been unlocked. I've been out there—I and my son here. And we brought something to show you."

He threw the wrapped parcel he had been carrying onto the table before Ebberly, holding on to a corner of the cloth that swaddled it. It struck heavily, rolled, and lay still, uncovered.

It was the dust-scarred, gold-plated shape of the Alpha Centauri probe, which had lost contact with the instruments watching it from the solar system eight years before.

Ebberly's hands were motionless on the pens. Slowly he lowered his gaze to the table, his face changing, and stared at the golden shape that lay before him there.

"You've lost, Ebberly," said Johnny. All about him, suddenly, the air of the room seemed to be filled with a soundless singing like that of wires tautened finally to the breaking point. "But only if you think the world going smash is the only alternative to your dream. There's a great future waiting for you as well as everybody else, if you can only step back from the edge of the Armageddon of a Sea-Land war that's facing us here, and adjust to a new sort of future."

He stood, watching the Transportation Baron. With the Space Swimmer, Blue Counselor, out beyond the stars, he had danced the dance of life. Now, here, on the other side of the coin, began a dance of death of which only he was aware, and with the future of all living human beings at stake.

"There's still time, Ebberly," Johnny said.

"You've lost, but you're only one ashore who has, if you can grow up and manage to face up to it. If you can do that, then it's the Land and Sea, together, that have won."

# 19

"Lost . . . ?" said Ebberly.

His face seemed to have fallen in on itself into a mask of savagery. The freckled skin had thinned and drawn tight, so that beneath it the heavy bones stood out like the fierce, animal skull of a predator, like the wolf, or leopard seal. His eyes, focused down on the golden shape before him were flat and opaque with little flecks of light, like glitters from the facets of a cut and polished stone:

"Lost?" he said again. "Me?"

He ground the second word to powder between his square teeth. "This is *my* world! It was my world the day I first opened my eyes on it, before you came into it, and it's been my world ever since! Its people do as I say they do. Its future goes as I say it goes. And when it stops being my world, it'll be nothing! A dead hunk of rock spinning under the moon!''

His eyes lifted and burned at Johnny with the fire outside of reason.

"You and your son!" He spat the words out, in fragments before him. "So you found a way to the stars? A way that's not my way? And more will go, will they? Tell me—where'll they find the ships to go in?"

"We don't need ships," said Johnny, meeting the wild, china-blue eyes steadily. "It's the way people dreamed about, since the dawn of time. Flying—with nothing but magnetic envelopes to enclose air around us—flying between the stars."

"Yes," snarled Ebberly. "Two of you. *Two* of you. You and your kid. And who led the way— who was necessary? Not you only. Or you'd have done it by yourself, long ago. It's your son—the boy here—that's important, isn't it, Joya? Not you. So you haven't got a space-road, yet, have you? And my own way to the stars is still waiting for me. You've got a key to them—that's all. A freak key to a freak route. And until you've had time to grow more keys like your kid, you still don't own the stars! And time you don't have!—Isn't that right?"

"The way you think of it," said Johnny, steadily, "yes."

"So take away your key and I win after all!" shouted Ebberly. He hunched forward. "Here's for your key then, exactly the way I planned it from the start—"

And he threw up both his hands as if surrendering.

"*Dad!*" cried Tomi. "*Look out!*"

For a moment Ebberly checked, hands still in the air, his eyes flickering incredulously from Tomi to Johnny and back again. In that split-second, Johnny's hand, thrusting out, knocked the boy away from the spot where Tomi had been standing and stepped himself onto that same spot, putting his own body between Ebberly and Tomi.

In the same moment Ebberly broke out of his hesitation and his thick hands slammed down on the two pencils. And, from underneath the table before him, in line with each pointing pencil leaped the two thin streams of fire, the positive and minus arcs of the powerful units designed to blow the heavy magnetic shields protecting fortresses, such as Stuve's tower at the hunting lodge had been.

Together, the twin fire-streams converged like two needle-thin bolts of red-yellow lightning upon Johnny's crouching and shielding figure.

# 20

In the sudden eruption of those two streams of light, all other power in the room was blown. The overhead floating lights went out and the windows' unnatural darkness winked away to show the pale sky of dawn, which lit up the wild and staring face of Ebberly, and the two leaping bolts.

These came together at a point upon the outer magnetic envelope enclosing Johnny. But not with the result that had been planned. Even as they reached that point where Tomi's chest would have been, they found Johnny's hands already upflung with the reflexes of the sea-born and the calculation of the mind that had built the original analog. Those hands were fitted together like the hands of a baseball catcher; and the two ripping streams of energy came together at a single point at the hands' combined center.

At that point the joined streams struck against the outer shield of the double magnetic envelope Johnny wore, penetrating to spread out, overload, and blow the envelope as such energy weapons were designed to do. But in penetrating the outer envelope and attempting to spread, the energy streams sought to slip between the outer and the inner envelope that still existed, untouched.

Only—there was no space between the two envelopes for them to occupy. As ordinary space-time did not intrude on the space-roads that were the linear subforces of the galaxy's magnetic field; so it could not intrude into the subforce interspace between the two magnetic envelopes. And the energy streams, being space-time elements, could not intrude either. The magnetic fields deflected all forces and pressures at right angles to their surfaces; and in Johnny's cupped palms the inner magnetic envelope had field surface projecting into space-time beyond the point of impact of the energy streams on the outer envelope.

The surfaces of both fields were perfectly smooth, frictionless, and automatically self-balancing. In Johnny's palms they swirled one above the other into a shape presenting a surface like a parabolic mirror, in which the joined energy forces were caught, pooled, and reflected.

In the sudden dawn-brightness of the room, the impinging streams were trapped and thrown back in a single beam, like a glancing ray of light from the sighting beam of a sonic rifle, from Johnny's cupped palms against the freckled forehead of Ebberly.

Ebberly was flung backward in his chair by the

sudden, galvanic reflexes of his muscles. —The beam winked out leaving him there. Silence rang in the room like the silence that rings through the standing timber, as when some great, reaching pine has just been cut down and come crashing to the earth. And, as in a forest, those standing around saw each other's faces fresh and strange and small against the new light of a day in which so much height and weight could be brought tumbling to simple earth.

"Kai . . .?" said Wally Kutch, in a shaking, uncertain voice. He lifted one fat hand uncertainly as if to touch the freckled wrist lying still on the table by his own, then dropped his hand again.

For there was no doubt. Only the dawn light flooding white and new through the wall-long window upon the silent and watching People of the Sea, and of the Land.

The thick-shouldered, brindle-haired figure of Ebberly sat motionless but still upright in his chair. Except that he did not move, and except for the knowledge that flooded the room, a casual glance might have deceived some of them, like Wally Kutch, into thinking that Kai still lived. But it was an illusion only, caused by Ebberly's upright posture in the chair. He sat leaning back against the backrest, his head against its top edge, his chin a little tilted upwards, his eyes closed.

He looked as if caught in a moment of thought, and arrested there.

But even as they stood watching, that moment in which it had all happened, in which time had seemed many times stretched so that so much could happen in so little interval, passed away

from them into all things finished. Into history,
the bottomless past from which nothing gone
could ever return. And the time sense of the
watchers drifted, contracted, slowing to a normal
pace again. They stirred, and looked about as if
seeing each other with unfamiliar eyes.

"Tomi—" said Johnny, turning to the boy.
"You're all right?"

"All right . . ." began Tomi and broke off to
blink and yawn uncontrollably. His eyes were
puffed with tiredness; and it came back to Johnny
that the boy had been going on stimulants for
some hours now.

"Hang on," said Johnny. "We'll be heading
back to sea, soon."

"Yes . . ." muttered Tomi, drowsily.

"He knew!"

Johnny turned back to the table at the sound of
the voice. It had been Ed Poira speaking, the
hard-bunched features of his face smoothed out
and flattened in an expression of awe.

"Your boy knew!" repeated Poira. "He called
out before Kai started to do anything!"

"Yes," said Johnny, "there are physiological
changes in the human body before any action is
taken—preparatory actions of the brain and nerve
and muscle cells. These changes alter the signals
put out by the magnetic fields of the cells in the
body. Tomi's sensitive to such signals. He can
read them—that's why he can talk to sea creatures. . . . and Space Swimmers. But never mind
that, now." He smiled grimly at Poira. "I asked
Tomi to warn me when Ebberly made up his mind
to attack either one of us—before Tomi and I came
in here."

Poira stared back at him. The Sea Captains, with Maytig, had moved in ominously, to stand beside Johnny and the boy, so that the two groups faced each other now only across the narrow barrier of the table. In the second of silence following Johnny's answer, Wally Kutch sighed, and stirred.

He had been sitting, staring at the upright body of Ebberly. Now, without taking his eyes off the dead man, he fumbled out of his shirt pocket the large, white handkerchief he carried there to wipe the corners of his mouth. Shaking it out, he stood up stiffly and turned to Ebberly.

Carefully, almost tenderly, he laid the handkerchief over Ebberly's head so that the dead face was covered. He sighed a little again, and sat back down in his own chair, knotting his hands together on the surface before him. Staring at nothing, he kneaded his old, fat hands together like someone cold, or in silent pain.

"Yes," said Poira, bitterly and hoarsely. He, like the rest had been watching the old man; but now he turned back to Johnny. "So you've won. What happens to the rest of us? We're going to be your underdogs ashore—that's the new Game, isn't it?"

Johnny opened his mouth—but Maytig spoke quickly, before him.

"No," she answered, looking directly into the dark eyes of Poira. "The Sea was all. We never wanted anything else. We'll go back to it now; and if you on shore just leave us alone there, you'll never even know we share the world with you. We're evolving away from you; and we've got a different way to go—"

"No," interrupted Johnny. "No, Maytig. No."
She checked, turning to stare at him.

"We're going no different way from the Land,"
said Johnny. "That's why we didn't have any right
to use the Ring of Fire against the people ashore.
Pat was right. Land and Sea are at an evolutionary
break-point, all right; but they've come to it together. It's just that four generations of sea-living
have reawakened necessary, ancient sensitivities
in us that the Land has had dulled and forgotten."

"Johnny!" It was Pat's voice. Pat was on his feet
at the end of the table and his face was alight.
"You know—? You've found proof the People are
still one with the Land?"

Johnny nodded, slowly.

"Proof," he answered, "in the shape of some
answers from one of the older Space Swimmers.
He'd been through it—the way all life forms go
through it, if they live long enough and keep on
evolving."

"Answers?" said Poira. He all but glared at
Johnny, in disbelief. "From a Space Bat."

"—Swimmer. Call them Swimmers from now
on," said Johnny. "They're as civilized as we humans, at comparable ages. In spite of the fact that
they're about as different from us as any life form
can be; and the fact that they can't conceive of our
way of life any better than we can conceive of
theirs. But I had Tomi there to interpret for me;
and I got my answers. They're born as nothing
more than clouds of living gas; and they evolve as
individuals, over fantastic time spans by our
reckoning, individually into intelligence. But
those who've evolved far enough know about this
same break-point in evolution we're at here on

Earth because they had to go through it themselves."

"What break-point?" asked Maytig, beside him now. He glanced down at her. The shock was draining from her face and her eyes were coming alive and penetrating.

"The cross-over point between the stages of conscious and unconscious evolution," he said. "It's a cross-over that's signalized by the development of an evolutionary ethic." He smiled a little wryly at her. "That's why the older Space Swimmers wouldn't talk to the young ones, or to Tomi. The younger ones can't possibly understand what the older ones are concerned with, until they develop the ethic on their own. Because they have to do it on their own—it can't be taught. But once a creature has it he begins to see the way to pass from unconscious to conscious control of his evolutionary development."

"Ethic?" demanded Poira; and Wally Kutch, seated beside the dead Ebberly, lifted his face to stare half-comprehendingly for the first time since Ebberly's death, at Johnny. "What is this ethic?" demanded Poira. "What's this business of controlling our own evolution? I never heard of it."

"You didn't listen in the right places then; and you didn't read," answered Johnny. "As far back as 1964 men like Hudson Hoagland, writing in Science magazine, was pointing out the unique possibilities of Man's being able to direct and control his own evolution."

He stopped speaking and glanced up and down the table on both sides. The faces of Maytig and the Sea Captains showed a dawning light of comprehension. The faces of the Barons, however, were still dark with a lack of understanding. Only Pat's face seemed to show that his mind had already leaped ahead to the point Johnny had been laboring to explain.

"I don't understand . . . I don't understand it," whimpered Wally Kutch out of the silence. "Now your boy here will go out, flying around between the stars. But what good is it? And meanwhile, what's going to happen with the rest of us? What'll we do now? Kai dead . . . everybody all mixed up. I don't know . . ." His voice muttered off into quiet. His old hands twisted together restlessly.

"Tomi won't be roaming the star-roads for some years yet," said Johnny, glancing at the boy, who was now literally asleep on his feet.

"Not . . .?" It was Pat speaking, finally as puzzled as the rest of them. "What'll he be doing, then, Johnny?"

Johnny looked back at him, squarely.

"He'll be coming ashore," Johnny said. "To live. And so will the rest of our fourth generation of the sea-born."

# 21

<hr />

"Our sea-children?" It was almost a cry of pain from Maytig. "After all we've done to make the sea safe for them to grow up in?"

"The rest of them— except Tomi," said Johnny, "can have a year or two of freedom in the surface and shallow waters yet. But then they'll be coming ashore." He looked directly, if sympathetically, at her. "You see—we're none of us, including Tomi, ready for the star-roads yet."

"But, Tomi . . ." began Maytig.

"The mature Space Swimmers wouldn't talk to him when he was alone. Remember?" Johnny asked her. "He handles the roads, but he's not grown up yet, any more than the young Space Swimmers are. He's got to mature and develop the evolutionary ethic on his own, first. As the older Swimmers know, it can't be taught—any more

than you can teach artistry to a painter or a composer. Everyone who develops it has to dig it out
on his own—in the case of the ethic, that means
understanding and responsibility for himself and
the future of his own kind."

He looked from her to Pat and back to Maytig
again.

"You understand, don't you?" he said. "Oh,
Tomi could go out there now and roam around
with the younger Swimmers, the way he's been
roaming around with Conquistador and Baldur in
the sea. But he doesn't really belong out there, yet.
He's a member of a race that's always fought to
grow upwards, instead of drifting along until
sheer weight of time brought each member of it
into the future singly and apart. If Tomi went out
on the space-roads as he is now, after a while he'd
get bored and come back to Earth on his own. As
he is, he'd find nothing to do out there."

"But if he grows up here, what then?" Pat
asked. "Why should it make any difference to
him, then?"

"Children play at things," Johnny said. "But
adults work at them. That's the difference. There's
work to be done out there, but not for children.
The roads require mature human beings."

"Work? What kind of work?" asked Pat.

"What kind of work . . ." echoed Johnny.

And suddenly, with those four words, it was all
with him again, as it had been for that split-
second in the berg-Home when he had touched
the shoulder of Tomi, and his long mental search
had ended. Vast, complex, reaching out beyond
comprehension like the space-roads themselves,
he glimpsed again the pattern of time and man

plunging far and far into the future until the mind could no longer follow it.

"The work of gods," he heard himself answering, out of the inconceivable complex of the pattern that surrounded him. As he heard himself say it, the pattern locked and held. All at once he was free to view it or to step away from it as he chose, and he knew then that he had it for good; that it would not disintegrate as the original analog had shattered into probabilities; that it would be there always, from now on, whenever he wished to see and touch and enter it again.

But on the heels of this came sudden understanding. —That he was going too fast for the others, that he was trying to take them beyond the depth and pressures of understanding they could tolerate, as yet—even Maytig and Pat, among the sea-People. His own words about the work of gods rang in his ears and he came back to the room his mind had left on the soft wings of caution.

"Gods?" Poira was growling. "What kind of gods?"

"There's only one kind of god—by definition," Johnny answered him, unexcitedly. "That's a being with no limit to his individual powers. And only a god can be such a being, because only a god can be trusted to have the god-like restraint necessary not to abuse such powers."

He glanced at Pat and saw his cousin, at least was understanding.

"That's the law of the evolutionary ethic," said Johnny. "You have to accept the ethic itself before you can derive from it the powers the ethic permits. You can't reject the self-restraint and self-discipline that it imposes without blinding yourself to the possibilities such self-control of evolution implies. In short, you can't have what the ethic gives without accepting the ethic itself first. Only by holding firmly to the ethic in everything do you go up and up, until—"

He broke off, checking himself to caution, again.

"Until . . ." prompted Pat after a second. "Until what?"

"I don't really know," said Johnny quietly, "—yet. I only know that there's something up there at the far end of the evolutionary ladder, waiting for us—some step even bigger than the one we're facing now. The Space Swimmer I talked to knew it, too—because he mentioned it on his own without my suggesting it—" he quoted softly, half to himself, " '. . . and afterwards, no more falling. But a long climb to the new light, beyond which there is no seeing until you pass over through it—and are gone . . .' "

He stopped speaking. No one else spoke. Even among the Barons there was no more speaking, and the pale, new daylight washing over them from the windows seemed to carry the truth of his words into all their inner selves and leave it marked upon their faces.

"But what now?" asked Pat, at last.

Johnny nodded.

"Now, it really begins," he said. "Sea and Land are going to have to become one human social unit again. The children of the future will have to be born and spend their early years in the cradle of the ocean. In the Sea they'll become aware of the instincts and senses the Sea brings out in us—and that on the most primitive level the space-roads require. There, in the Sea, they'll grow the strong, true link with this world that will anchor them against the shock of any knowledge to come; and teach them freedom and independence and searching minds as a birthright so basic it's simply taken for granted . . ."

He broke off once more, for the picture was forming in his mind and unrolling itself before him as he spoke. Clear as the memory of his own childhood he saw the ever-moving ocean of the future and the shallow reef and shore waters peopled with the free young swimmers.

"Do you see it?" he asked, turning to the seaborn.

"I think so . . ." said Maytig, thoughtfully.

"I see it," said Pat. His eyes glowed darkly. Already, the music of the years to come was sounding in his mind. A French horn called across the unceasing surface of the Sea, and trumpets answered it from mountain heights ashore. While far off, above the sky, there was the first whisper of strings calling the children of the human race further than even imagination had gone before.

". . . After they've grown in the Sea, they'll come ashore," Johnny went on. "The Land and all its history, all it can teach them that's been done, is as necessary to them as the Sea. Then, finally, when Sea and Land together have brought them to the point of developing, on their own, the evolutionary ethic, then—one by one—they'll take to the star-roads, where their work will really begin." The images of his words glowed in him as Pat's eyes were glowing.

"Out there," he heard himself saying, "they'll

search the secrets of our universe. They'll find ways of getting off the star-roads down to the surfaces of other worlds. They'll find means for passing the very hearts of stars. They'll explore the galaxy and go out beyond to other island universes. They will go, and do, and meet—whatever is there to be met. Because this is just the beginning; this world is like the egg from which we've just been hatched and all the rest of existence hangs waiting for us, out there, beyond."

"I don't know why . . ." stammered Wally Kutch. His fat, aging hands, at last unclasped, were trembling on the table before him. He stared down at them as if they were rebellious, independent creatures and he helpless to control them. "Why do that? Why leave Earth anyway? What's out there for anyone to leave here, home, where they belong?"

The room was silenced again. Not even Johnny answered immediately. The old man's voice had a quavering, questioning cry in it that struck fairly into them all.

"I don't know," said Johnny, for a second time. "There's no telling what's out there. But we'll go. We'll go—everyone knows we'll have to go, because it's in us to go. It's how we're made."

"It's always been that way," said Pat, leaning toward the trembling old man. "From the first man hanging to a branch where he was safe and looking out, away out, across the treeless plain at a far line of mountains. Just shapes, misty and distant, and beyond a place where there were no more trees to climb and be safe in. But he had to go—he had to go—and so will we."

"The world won't change so fast in your time,"

said Johnny, gently, looking across the table at Wally Kutch. "It's not for you, anyway—you're past the time. It's for the young of each generation, coming new and new every twenty years or less into the front line of the assault."

He straightened up and looked up and down the table at Poira and the other Barons. His voice became brisk.

"Suppose the Sea Captains and I meet with you all here in six weeks?" he said. "That'll give us time to break the news in Sea and on Land, both. Then, when we get together again, we can begin to talk about the changes that'll have to be made. The groups that'll have to be set up to study how the changes will be made. We can arrange a joint Land-and-Sea controlling body to begin with. —Does that sound all right?"

"All right," said Poira, flatly and a little numbly. The rest at the table sat without words. With Ebberly dead, it seemed silently agreed by the Barons that Poira should lead them.

"Then, here we go—home," said Johnny. He reached out and gently shook Tomi's shoulder. The boy's eyes blinked open and he straightened groggily up from the table edge against which he had been leaning. "Tomi—Maytig. Sea-People. Let's go home!"

He headed for the exit. The other sea-born fell in behind him. Out of the corner of his eye he saw Pat come around the end of the table to follow also— and Mila Jhan jumped up from her seat and ran after Pat.

Together they went out the door and clattered down the escalator ramp, and out through the empty Terminal Building, now pinkly lit by the rising sun. They went out the front entrance of the building and down to the sea-level pier holding the ranks of ducted flyers that stood as silent and empty now as exhibits in a museum. They followed the path that Pat had followed six months before, until they came to the end of the concrete pier where he had taken to the Sea.

"The smallboats are on automatic, two fathoms deep, about two hundred yards out," said Maytig as they halted at the Sea's edge. "We'll have to swim out. Do you want me to help you with Tomi?"

Johnny shook his head. The boy was leaning against him, now that they had stopped moving and was drifting off to sleep again. Johnny grinned down at him.

"I'll handle him," he told Maytig. The Sea Captains around them were already pulling up the facemasks of their waterlungs and taking to the morning-bright blue waves that lapped at the edge of the concrete platform.

"I'm going with you," the voice of Mila said behind Johnny. He and Maytig looked around to see Mila's face set in stubborn lines as she talked to Pat. "I can swim two hundred yards. If I can't, it's time I learned."

Pat smiled, shook his head, and stopped her with one hand as she started to reach down to take off the one shoe she still had on. The other shoe was already clutched in her right hand.

"Later," he said. "I'll take you to sea later on, if you want. But for now, let's both stay on shore. For some time you and I've been liaison between the Sea and the Land. That's why we've been useful. Let's go on doing it a while longer. I just came down here myself to see them all off."

Mila hesitated. Slowly, she began to put back on the one shoe she had taken off.

Pat turned to Johnny. They looked at each other without feeling any great need for words, after the fashion of the sea-born. Johnny felt Maytig close beside him. Her shoulder brushed warmly against the skin of his upper right arm. Tomi leaned heavily against him on the other side. For the first time all of them left on the pier felt released, enclosed and surrounded by a sort of human warmth held all in common, like the warmth of a family together.

The voices of birds sounded unexpectedly overhead. They looked up to see a high-flying flock of whistling swans, once thought to be drifting into extinction, but now regaining their numbers, in migration now northward with the spring. The swans passed, graceful as white dreams, leaving their wild, free voices trailing down from the sky behind them. The four adults below lowered their eyes and looked at each other again.

"Well, Pat . . ." said Johnny. He smiled. "We came through it all right. And"—he closed his hand around the hand of Maytig beside him—" better than I sometimes thought we might. We've got full lives ahead of us now. It looks interesting."

"Yes," said Pat. He smiled too, but a little sadly. The note of the whistling swans had sounded deeper within him than in any of the others. It echoed there now to another note—the lonely twilight note of a bull's horn at the lips of a prehistoric, fur-clad herdsman, calling from the mountain hillside down through shadows to a valley at the day's end.

"But it's a lot of centuries we're leaving behind us," said Pat, "and that the world's leaving behind it. All the past that started in a tree, or a hole in a hill some hundreds of thousands of years ago. Now, here we are standing at the end of the history of Man on Earth."

"No," said Johnny. "Only at the end of the old history. The new is just beginning to be written."

"I suppose." Pat nodded. "But I guess, being human, I'd like to have both—to keep the old and have the new as well."

"Who knows?" said Johnny, smiling again. "Maybe, in the end, some other hundreds of thousands of years from now, that's what we'll have. Right now, the future's waiting."

He lifted a hand to Pat and Mila and turned toward the water. The Sea Captains had already gone. He pulled up Tomi's facemask over the boy's mouth and nose, then pulled up his own. He shook Tomi momentarily awake and dove cleanly into the waves before the pier. Tomi and Maytig followed him.

The trail of exhaust bubbles from their masks stretched away south by east, out toward the endless sea horizon and the bright sky of morning. Above the horizon the sun was rising fast. As Pat and Mila stood watching, those three last trails of bubbles ran outward toward the light—until they, themselves, were turned into bubbles of light, and lost to sight in the coming day that was now flooding Sea and Sky and Land with an unquenchable illumination.

> Has my chained spirit, listening,
> Heard calls beyond Earth's bars?
> Of the great Space Swimmers, schooling,
> On their roads between the stars?

> I have heard them, and I hear them—
> Those who do not know small years;
> And the bars are dust behind me,
> As I lift to greet my peers!

# Gordon R. Dickson

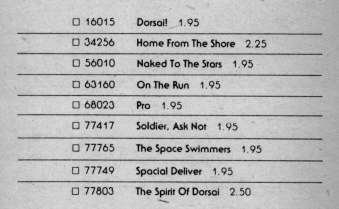

☐ 16015    Dorsai!   1.95

☐ 34256    Home From The Shore   2.25

☐ 56010    Naked To The Stars   1.95

☐ 63160    On The Run   1.95

☐ 68023    Pro   1.95

☐ 77417    Soldier, Ask Not   1.95

☐ 77765    The Space Swimmers   1.95

☐ 77749    Spacial Deliver   1.95

☐ 77803    The Spirit Of Dorsai   2.50

# H. Beam Piper

☐ 24890 **Four Day Planet/Lone Star Planet** $2.25

☐ 26192 **Fuzzy Sapiens** 1.95

☐ 48492 **Little Fuzzy** 1.95

☐ 49052 **Lord Kalvan Of Otherwhen** 1.95

☐ 77781 **Space Viking** 1.95

*Available wherever paperbacks are sold or use this coupon.*